I0571911

THE LEGEND OF
JUDGMENT ROCK
AND OTHER
MYSTERY STORIES

SHARON LOVE COOK

"Bluefish Weather" appeared in Alfred Hitchcock's Mystery Magazine, December 1997; *"Family Pride"* appeared in Orchard Press Mystery Magazine, June 2000; *"A Marriage Made in Heaven"* appeared in Over My Dead Body, October, 2011; *"The Legend of Judgment Rock"* appeared in Great Mystery and Suspense Magazine, Winter, 2006; *"The Ghost of Winthrop Hall,"* nonfiction, appeared in Haunted Encounters: Real Life Experiences of Supernatural Experiences, Atriad Press, 2003; *"Men of Means"* appeared in Austin Layman's Crimestalker Casebook, Spring 2007

Neptune Rising Press

Copyright © 2012 Sharon Love Cook

All rights reserved.

ISBN: 0615669719

ISBN-13: 9780615669717

THE LEGEND OF JUDGMENT ROCK
AND OTHER
MYSTERY STORIES

COVER ILLUSTRATION
BY SHARON LOVE COOK

CONTENTS

"THE LEGEND OF JUDGMENT ROCK"

"Dorothy, did you take the last piece of apple tart?" Vivian Crimp examined the empty plate scattered with crumbs.

"Mrs. Crimp, it sat there for three days. I figured—"

Vivian raised her hand, silencing her. "You are paid to clean, Dorothy, not to figure. The terms of your employment were laid out—one half hour for lunch, which you will bring from home."

Dorothy bit her lip. "I understand, Mrs. Crimp, but Tuesday morning I didn't have time to make lunch. My husband's breathing worried me awful and . . ."

Mrs. Crimp stared at her housekeeper until the woman fell silent. In a quieter tone she said, "Let's not discuss this again. I'll be at my office, should anyone call."

When she heard the front door close, Dorothy sighed and lifted the heavy plastic bucket into the sink. Time to wash the kitchen tiles. Although they were spotless, Mrs. Crimp was a psychic when it came to finding the tiniest smudge.

She turned on the hot water. If she finished early, she'd call Harold at home. . . .

Sitting behind the wheel of her gleaming Saab, Vivian Crimp paused to glance back at the house. She wondered if Dorothy was on the phone.

Her housekeeper had one sob story after another regarding her husband's health. Vivian would fire her in a minute if she had a replacement. Unfortunately, Granite Cove was typical of small New England towns; its people weren't to be trusted.

She headed down the long driveway, still mulling over her earlier confrontation with Dorothy. The apple tart was the last straw. A piece of pastry today, a diamond ring tomorrow. In any case, it wasn't Vivian's fault her housekeeper was struggling. If she didn't waste her money on cheap take-out food, she would have something to bank.

Vivian shook her head. It did no good to point this out; some people were basically ignorant. She pressed the accelerator. The Saab's tires spun, leaving a spray of pebbles in her wake.

It was late afternoon when Mrs. Crimp returned, parking in the center of the circular driveway. In the waning light her house looked like something out of *Town & Country*. Its solid granite facade gave the impression of a medieval fortress, while the leaded windows revealed nothing. Surrounding the house, mammoth rocks worn smooth by pounding waves kept the Atlantic at bay.

It was an impressive piece of property; most impressive was the fact that she, a widow, owned it outright.

As she gazed at her house, the front door opened. Dorothy appeared, ushering out a pair of middle-age women. So engrossed were they in conversation, they jumped when Vivian slammed the car door.

"What can I do for you ladies?" she called, locking up the Saab.

Dorothy rushed forward, wringing her hands. "Mrs. Crimp, these ladies are from the library committee. They're raising money for a—"

"I was addressing them, Dorothy. I'd like to know what they're doing in my house."

The pair exchanged glances and the smaller woman stepped forward. "Mrs. Crimp, don't blame your housekeeper. We're canvassing the neighborhood, raising money for a children's room at the library. We thought you, a newcomer, would want to be part of it."

Vivian removed her sunglasses and stared at the women. "Why would you assume that? If I'm not mistaken, doesn't the library already have a children's room?"

The second woman spoke up. "It's a basement room that floods every spring–a damp, unhealthy environment for the little ones."

A crevice appeared between Vivian's eyebrows. "If you ask me there's too much handed to children today. They're not willing to work for anything."

"In that case, Mrs. Crimp, perhaps you'll buy a ticket to our literary event. A local historian will read from his latest book. You, especially will want to hear the legend of Captain Hackett."

"Why would I care about that?" Vivian said.

The visitors exchanged glances. "Do you mean you're not familiar with the story surrounding your house?"

"What is it, some local foolishness?"

"You might call it foolish, but folks around here believe it. Even today, fishermen stay clear of Judgment Rock."

"What on earth is Judgment Rock?"

"It's that giant boulder behind your house," the woman said. "The story is romantic, yet very sad."

Vivian longed to be rid of the meddlesome pair. However, a local legend might be just the thing to amuse her city friends. She set her briefcase on the ground. Crossing her arms over her chest, she said, "Go ahead then, tell me."

The woman took a deep breath and began: "In the mid-1800s, Captain Josiah Hackett made his fortune in West Indian rum. He was a tyrant, they say. The only men who'd sign onto his ship were convicts. In any event, upon reaching mid life he decided it was time to marry.

"One day he spotted Lily, a beautiful young girl working at the village tavern. She was an orphan, her sailor father having died of a ruptured appendix during a long voyage. Shortly after, Lily's mother died in childbirth. The tavern owner, taking pity on the girl, allowed her to live in the wine cellar in exchange for chores. Along with a few handouts from the church, Lily got by.

"Before long, Captain Hackett asked Lily to marry him. Although he was twenty-five years older and not pleasant to look at, she accepted. After the captain built his house high on the rocks, he forbade his bride to leave. He was an extremely jealous, suspicious man. The tradespeople visiting the house claimed that Lily sat all day at her bedroom window looking out to sea.

"To celebrate their first wedding anniversary, Captain Hackett decided to have his wife's portrait painted. Someone suggested an artist from Boston, who'd created a name for himself. The artist, a handsome young man, visited Captain Hackett's household during that long winter while Lily sat for him. Finally, in early spring, the painting was finished. It is rumored that Lily, upon seeing her portrait, wept. Some claim it was because she'd forgotten how lovely she was; others say it was because the portrait was finished.

"After the young man returned to Boston, Captain Hackett hung the portrait in his bedroom, away from the public's eye. In the meantime, he pressured Lily for heirs.

"The days passed. One night near Summer's end, two fishermen spotted a rowboat pulling up outside the captain's house, around midnight. A woman appeared at an upper window. She tossed out a rope and proceeded to climb down. Upon reaching the ground, she threw herself into the man's arms.

"Minutes later, the pair boarded the rowboat. As they rowed away, the moon appeared from behind the clouds. It cast its light upon Captain Hackett, who stood high on Judgment Rock. He threw a barrage of rocks at the little boat. Many hit their mark.

"Though the couple paddled frantically, the rowboat took on water. In the end, it was like a toy, sucked into the dark, swirling sea. When it vanished, Captain Hackett threw his head back and laughed. The terrible sound echoed over the coast. The fishermen were so frightened they rowed to shore, panicked.

"Eventually, fragments of the rowboat washed on shore, but the bodies of Lily and her artist were never recovered. The police had little choice but to believe that Captain Hackett's wife and her lover had run away.

"As the years passed, Captain Hackett, with his long, gray beard, was often spotted on moonlit nights, standing on the big rock. After his death, sailors claimed they heard his ungodly laugh. As a result, local fishermen went out of their way to avoid the site. They claimed the ghost of Captain Hackett stood in judgment. Those who sailed past the rock had better have a clear conscience, else they'd end up on the bottom of the sea.

"In the Summer of 1925, a church group heading to a picnic on Baker's Island passed Judgment Rock. Not long after, their boat was capsized by a whale. Today, the legend continues."

Dorothy wiped her eyes. "No matter how often I hear that story, it makes me cry. That poor girl."

"Well I think it's ghastly," Mrs. Crimp said. "You people have nothing better to do than tell ghost stories." She picked up her briefcase. "If you'll excuse me, I have work to do." She gave Dorothy a dark look. "Unlike some people."

Inside the house, she made a beeline for her locked study. Without removing her coat, she went to her desk, unlocked a drawer, and removed a tan envelope. Sitting behind the desk, she carefully counted the thick wad of bills.

Satisfied that nothing was missing, she moved to a corner table. It held a half dozen bottles. She poured scotch into a heavy glass and drank, shuddering when the liquor hit her stomach. Glass in hand, she paced the room.

The situation with Dorothy had gone too far. Tomorrow, she'd have the locks changed, and Dorothy had to go. No doubt the library women with their ridiculous tales had been snooping among her valuables. She wouldn't be surprised if Dorothy was in cahoots with them.

She poured another drink. Instead of a calming effect, it made her more agitated. Imagine those women, she thought, wanting her money for a children's room. As a child, she hadn't had time to visit the library; she'd had chores. During college, on scholarship, she'd worked two jobs.

It wasn't until she met her husband that things changed. Victor was older and at the time, married. Together they built a successful business the old-fashioned way: buying inventory–cheap–from bankrupt companies.

Her reverie was interrupted by a knock on the door. Dorothy stood outside in a tattered raincoat, a rumpled scarf at her neck.

"Mrs. Crimp, I'm going to catch the early bus because of the storm." She stepped timidly into the room. "I want to apologize for those ladies. They weren't in but for five minutes. Didn't even sit down."

Vivian waved away the woman's remarks. "What did you prepare for my dinner?"

"Cold roast chicken. You might want to get more milk before the storm. My Harold says the downtown's packed with people buying up everything."

Vivian rolled her eyes. "Hysteria runs rampant in this town. By the way, what storm are you referring to?"

You didn't hear? A Northeaster's coming any minute. Big winds and high surf. I put your flashlight and some batteries in the pantry, just in case."

Vivian nodded. "Fine, Dorothy. Run along then."

Dorothy gripped the handle of her purse, reluctant to go. "Well, I'd better not miss that bus. See you tomorrow, Mrs. Crimp."

After Dorothy left, Vivian stuffed the money back into the envelope. Instead of putting it in the drawer, she tucked it inside her blouse. Later, she'd put it in the bedroom safe. After pouring another drink, she carried it to the living room, stopping before the French doors.

Outside, the sky and the ocean were dark. White capped waves spewing foam crashed on the rocks. On the terrace, an unfurled patio umbrella flapped noisily in the wind. She opened the door and peered at it, cursing Dorothy for her neglect. "Too busy entertaining the local gossips," she muttered, gulping the last of her drink. She would have to secure the umbrella herself.

She grabbed the flashlight from the pantry and moments later struggled to open the door against the wind. Outside, she made her way across the rain-slicked terrace. The waves sent sheets of foam over the rocks, spraying the flagstones. Gripping the metal railing surrounding the terrace she reached the umbrella. As she struggled to secure it, she heard a loud, grating noise. She aimed the flashlight at the lower rocks. There, a small white rowboat sat, pummeled by the waves. She gripped the railing and slowly descended the terrace steps to get a closer look.

She could see that the boat was stuck on the rocks. There was nothing she could do. When she turned back to the house, the lights went out. As she climbed the terrace steps, two shadowy figures appeared in the gloom. She aimed the flashlight at them. It was a man and woman, huddled together. Their clothes were soaking wet—*as if they'd been underwater!*

Slowly they approached. Panicked, she spun around. There was nowhere to escape; before her was the roaring sea. As the pair got closer, she ran, slipping and sliding to the big rock. Pulling herself up, her knuckles scraped the hard, wet surface. Her feet, clad in thin slippers, fumbled for a foothold. Yet inch by inch she rose up the face of the rock, too afraid to look back.

As she neared the summit, the heavy flashlight slipped and rolled into a crevice. She grabbed for it. In the process, her foot lost its hold and she slid, clawing at the moss covered surface.

Soon her hands were clawing the air.

"Would you like milk or cream in your tea?" the policeman asked Dorothy.

"Cream would be nice."

A sweet young man, she thought. What a shock it had been, seeing his cruiser in the driveway. And when he told her about Mrs. Crimp, she'd almost fainted. Now, calmer, she looked around the seaweed covered terrace. She'd have to dry the chair cushions in the sun before mildew set in.

The officer returned with her tea. "How are you feeling now?"

"Better," Dorothy said. "I'm just confused about the neighbors finding Mrs. Crimp. I didn't think she even knew them."

"It wasn't a social call," he said. "Their rowboat got loose and ended up on her rocks. When they came over to get it, they found her climbing the big rock."

Dorothy shook her head. "That's what I don't understand. Mrs. Crimp never went near those rocks."

The young man hesitated. "Was your employer in the habit of drinking a little too much?"

"You mean liquor? Mrs. Crimp liked a drink or two in the afternoon. . . ."

"Her blood alcohol level was high. That might explain it."

"You could be right," Dorothy said, uncertain.

He got to his feet. "I'm going to lock up now. Can I give you a lift?"

"I think I'll finish my tea, if that's all right with you. It's such a lovely day." She looked at the puddles of dirty water on the terrace. "If you'll leave the mop and bucket, I'll clean up here."

"There's not much point, ma'am."

"It's fine," she said. "Gives me a chance to say goodbye to this place." She looked out at the sea, sparkling like diamonds in the sun. "I'm sure going to miss it."

After the policeman left, Dorothy remained on the terrace. At any moment she expected Mrs. Crimp to appear at the window and accuse her of wasting time. She smiled to herself. Poor Mrs. Crimp. She had so much, yet was always scared somebody would take it away.

After a while Dorothy got to her feet. It was time to mop the terrace. As she knelt at the outdoor spigot, she spotted a section of mesh tangled in the seaweed below the big rock. It might be the inside of a lobster trap, she thought. During a storm they often broke loose.

She pulled off her shoes and slowly crossed the barnacle-covered rocks. Using the mop handle as a hook, she dragged the sodden mess onto dry rock. Pawing through clumps of kelp and moss, she found a water-logged envelope. When she pressed it with the heel of her hand, dark sea water gushed out. She opened the flap and discovered a thick wad of $100 bills inside. She stood and removed her apron, folding it around the soggy bundle. Back at the terrace, she slipped it inside her canvas tote.

When she finished swabbing the flagstones, she leaned the mop against the railing to dry in the sun. She glanced at her watch. The bus to town was leaving in 25 minutes. She had time to stop at the seafood take-out. She imagined Harold's surprise when she returned home with *two* large boxes of Essex fried clams.

Minutes later she headed down the long driveway, the tote bag over her arm. Nearing the end, she turned for a final glimpse of the house. As she did, a laugh rang out, echoing along the coast. It was a sad sound and she wasn't afraid. With her free hand, she waved goodbye.

"A MARRIAGE MADE IN HEAVEN"

Edith Bicknell heaved a sigh of relief when the last of the mourners said their goodbyes. She had instructed Florence to help the elderly guests with their wraps. Now she watched as the woman buttoned coats, tied scarves and all but pinched their withered cheeks before sending them out into the January twilight.

The old dears probably enjoy the attention, Edith reasoned. She returned to the kitchen to make sure the caterers hadn't make off with the good silver. Nonetheless, when Florence hadn't returned in ten minutes, Edith decided to search. Although the cleaning woman was a hard worker, she was easily distracted.

After hanging up her apron, Edith exited the kitchen. She passed the big, empty dining room. Outside the den, she stopped. Mr. Smithwick sat inside the dimly lit room, his white head sagging forward. Was he asleep or merely resting after the long afternoon? At the cemetery, he'd looked ready to topple over, cane and all.

She placed a hand on his shoulder. He looked up with reddened eyes. "What is it, Edith?"

"Pastor Chittick and the guests are gone, Mr. Smithwick. Why don't you go on up? Florence and I will finish down here."

He nodded. "Yes, I think I'll do that."

She stood aside as he struggled to his feet and shuffled to the staircase. At the bottom, he looked up. The sadness on his face was painful to see. She hurried from the room, continuing her search.

She finally discovered Florence outside tossing rock salt over the flag-stone path. "I need you in the kitchen," Edith said.

"In a minute," Florence said, her breath making white clouds in the night air. "A couple old birds almost went ass-over-teakettle out here. Mr. Smithwick doesn't need a law suit on top of losing his wife."

Edith pulled her sweater closer. "That's enough, Florence. Let's finish up inside and go home." As she spoke, a light shone upstairs in the big house. Mr. Smithwick's pale face appeared briefly at the window before the curtains closed.

"Poor thing," Florence said. "He'll miss her. That was a marriage made in heaven."

"Amen," Edith said. "Now let's get inside."

The following day, Edith arrived at noon. She found Mr. Smithwick in the den wearing a bathrobe over pajamas. Although the TV blared, the old man appeared to be dozing. When she lowered the volume, he woke with a start.

"It's just me, Mr. Smithwick. I'll fix you something nice for lunch."

"I'm not hungry, thank you."

"Have you eaten today?"

"I'm going upstairs," he said, reaching for his cane. When she moved to help, he waved her away.

"If you want anything special for dinner, leave me a note on the dining room table," she said. "I'm scheduled to work three days this week."

"There's nothing I want," he said, shuffling to the stairs.

That afternoon, Edith bustled about the kitchen. She was stirring a pot of lentil soup when the doorbell rang. "Better not be another florist," she muttered, wiping her hands. The living room was crammed with flowers. With Mr. Smithwick's approval, she'd take some to the local nursing home. Let others enjoy them, she thought. Mr. Smithwick hadn't even opened the cards.

A middle age woman in a tweed suit stood on the steps. Her copper colored hair blazed in the winter sun. In her gloved hands she held a pie. After a brisk, "Good afternoon," she pushed past Edith into the foyer.

"Excuse me," Edith said, eying the nervy stranger. "What can I do for you?"

"Are you the housekeeper?" the woman asked, her eyes taking in the wall of old family portraits in gilded frames. "I made this especially for Mr. Smithwick." She handed Edith the pie.

"I'm the cook," Edith said. "Who are you?"

"I'm Sandra Flint, an old friend of Mrs. Smithwick's, from the church."

"St. Agatha's?" Edith asked, surprised. Mrs. Smithwick's church friends had been older and more . . . reserved than Sandra Flint.

"That's right. I was new to the community when dear Marjorie took me under her wing." She dabbed at her eyes. "Now I'd like to pay my respects to Angus, I mean, Mr. Smithwick."

"He's resting."

"A shame." She opened her purse and removed an envelope. "Please see that he gets this."

Edith watched the woman leave, teetering in high heels on the snowy walkway. She got into a low-slung sports car and roared off, her tires kicking up flumes of snow. Edith stared down at the pastel pink envelope with *Angus* scrawled across the front.

It was an overcast Wednesday when Edith returned to the Smithwick house. Upon entering the pantry, she spotted Florence crouched at the kitchen door. "Are you snooping?"

Florence spun around, a finger to her lips. "Shh, he's got a visitor in the den."

"Who's got a visitor?"

"Mr. Smithwick. Some dame in a short skirt's reading to him."

"I don't meddle in my client's affairs," Edith said. "That goes for you as well."

"You're the boss," Florence said, reluctantly closing the door. "I'll be upstairs if you need me." Ten minutes later she returned to find Edith occupying the spot she'd vacated. "So, who's the dame?" she asked.

Edith spun around. "Don't creep up on me like that." She straightened her apron. "Her name is Sandra Flint. She was here on Monday with a pie she claimed was homemade, although I found a receipt stuck to the bottom of the pan."

"Are they still in the den?"

Edith nodded. "She's reading to him but I can't hear what it is."

"Why don't we walk past?"

"Too obvious." Edith frowned, thinking hard. "How about if we gather the funeral arrangements in the living room? Mr. Smithwick said it was all right."

"Let's go," Florence said.

"Now remember," Edith said, "don't gawk at them."

"You're the boss."

The women stopped outside the den. Inside, Mr. Smithwick in pajamas and bathrobe sat on the sofa next to his visitor, whose sheer stockings gleamed in the light from a table lamp.

"Excuse me, Mr. Smithwick . . ."

He looked up. "Yes, Edith?"

"If you don't mind, we'll collect the flowers to take to the nursing home."

"Take whatever you need."

Working silently, the pair soon filled the trunk of Edith's car. Back in the kitchen, she put the kettle on. "Let's have some tea to warm up."

"What's that she's reading?" Florence asked, scooping a mound of sugar into her cup.

"Scripture."

"I don't know beans about Scripture," Florence said, "but I know mischief, and that dame is mischief wrapped in a skirt."

"Let's not jump to conclusions," Edith said. "The woman's a member of the church. Perhaps it's nothing more than Christian kindness."

Florence snorted. "Maybe you didn't notice, but the last time we passed the den, her skirt was hiked up high."

Edith sighed. "I noticed."

"Listen, tomorrow I clean for Mrs. Wigglesworth. She was a good friend of Mrs. Smithwick's. I'll ask her about Sandra Flint."

"And I'll have a talk with my nephew, Roland," Edith said. "We're meeting for dinner. Roland's head of security at the college, a resourceful lad."

Roland Bicknell ladled duck sauce over pork fried rice and handed the bowl to his aunt sitting opposite him in the booth. "Personally, I think Mr. Smithwick should be left alone," he announced.

"He's not himself," Edith said. "The man relied on his wife for everything. He's lost without her, and it breaks my heart."

"If he's that rich he won't be lost for long," Roland said. "He'll find some nice widow."

"That I wouldn't mind," Edith said. "It's Sandra Flint that's got me worried. I don't trust her."

Roland smiled. "Now Auntie, you said she's only visited twice."

"True, but something tells me she's moving in—like a black widow spider. Will you look into her background?"

"Aunt Edith, you don't understand. The college security database is limited to students. That doesn't include Sandra Flint."

"I see." She glanced down at her plate. "I guess I'll have to tell Florence there's nothing we can do for poor old Mr. Smithwick . . ."

He sighed. "I've got a cop friend who owes me one after I got him a pass to the fitness center. Let me talk to him."

She took a slip of paper from her bag. "Here's Sandra's license plate number."

After dinner, their waiter set a tray containing two fortune cookies before them. Edith broke hers open and read the message: "Tend to your own needs before the needs of others."

"Appropriate," he said. "You're always fretting about me. Now it's Mr. Smithwick under your microscope."

"I don't fret about you, Roland. I promised my dear brother, rest his soul, I'd look after you. If you were involved with someone unsuitable, I'd feel obligated to intervene." She bit into the cookie. "By the way, *are* you involved with anyone?"

"No, and you'll be the first to know."

"Good. Now I must be going. Don't forget to speak to your police friend."

On Friday, Edith was surprised to find Mr. Smithwick in the living room, fully dressed, his coat over his lap. "Going out, are you?" she asked. "The car's been garaged so long I'm afraid the battery may be dead."

"I won't be needing it," he said. "Someone from the church is picking me up. We're visiting a granite company up north. I've decided to commission a memorial bench for my wife."

"What a lovely gesture," Edith said. "Is it your idea?"

"No, it was Ms. Flint's, and frankly, it's a corker."

The doorbell interrupted them.

"I'll see who it is," Edith said.

He stood up. "I'm going upstairs to grab a handkerchief."

Sandra Flint, in a form-fitting red suit, stepped uninvited into the foyer. She glanced into the living room. "I thought you took all the flowers to the nursing home."

"Not all of them. Mr. Smithwick wanted some as a reminder of his wife."

"Yes, they are rather dry, aren't they?"

Before Edith could respond, the old man appeared and warmly greeted his visitor. "Will you be returning for lunch?" Edith asked,

"We'll probably stop someplace for a bite." Turning to his companion, he said, "If that's all right with you, Sandra. I don't want to monopolize your time."

"Nonsense, Angus. The memorial bench project is my priority as well."

Edith watched them walk arm in arm to the car. From a distance, Mr. Smithwick didn't look that old at all . . .

The following week she was surprised to find him dressed and sitting at the dining room table. "You're up bright and early, sir."

"I was hoping for a bowl of your Irish porridge."

"Certainly. Cream and brown sugar?"

"Fine, and while you're at it, fix another place setting. Ms. Flint is joining me for breakfast."

"I see," she said. "I'm glad your appetite's improved."

Florence pounced on her the minute she stepped into the kitchen. "That's not the only thing that's improved." She reached into her apron pocket and pulled out a thin gold hoop. "Look at this."

"What is it?" Edith asked.

"An earring. Wanna know where I found it?"

"I'm afraid to ask . . ."

"Upstairs. In his bed."

"Oh no." Edith clamped a hand to her mouth.

"That dame works faster than a flock of sea gulls at a clam bake. Let's contact Mr. Smithwick's son and tell him what's happening."

"It won't do any good. Elliott's off in the Galapagos on a research ship. By the way, did you speak to Mrs. Wigglesworth?"

"Uh huh. When I asked if Sandra Flint had been a friend of Mrs. Smithwick's, the old dame looked like she smelled something bad. 'Hardly,' she said."

"I'm not surprised," Edith said. "Now I've got to get to work. Her ladyship's coming for breakfast."

When Edith returned with a breakfast tray, Sandra Flint was already seated in the dining room. "That smells delicious," Mr. Smithwick said. "Sandra, you must try Edith's marvelous porridge."

"Just toast for me," she said.

Edith nodded and moved to the pantry. There she heard Mr. Smithwick ask, "What was the name of that drink you made last night?"

"It's called 'Peaches & Dreams.' Did you like it?"

"Loved it. I hope I didn't nod off. You must find me terribly dull."

Edith waited for a response and hearing nothing, opened the door a crack. She spotted Sandra Flint leaning across the table to kiss the old man's cheek.

After breakfast, the couple donned their coats.

"Will you be back for lunch, Mr. Smithwick?" Edith asked.

"Probably not," he said, turning to his companion. "Where are we headed today?"

"Portsmouth, New Hampshire," she said, smoothing his coat lapels.

"We're visiting another granite quarry," he told Edith. "Tracking down the finest stone."

As Edith watched the couple drive away, she wondered if Florence was also observing them. Her suspicions were confirmed by a loud clatter on the stairs followed by Florence racing into the room and shouting, "We gotta call the Coast Guard, find that ship Mr. Smithwick's son is on."

"It's thousands of miles away. The only communication is ship-to-shore radio."

"Darn it! What about your nephew, Roland? Did he learn anything?"

"He left a message. Apparently the background check is taking longer than expected."

"In the meantime, that dame's got Mr. Smithwick wrapped tighter than a canned ham."

Edith nodded. "I can't argue with that."

The following week Edith worked in the Smithwick kitchen stocking the freezer with homemade soups and casseroles, all carefully labeled. As Mr. Smithwick was often out, they communicated through notes. His last read: *Please prepare something special tonight–dinner for two.*

On Wednesday, her day off, Edith attended a matinee in Boston. Arriving home, she found a message from Florence telling Edith to call the minute she got in. "Is something wrong?" Edith asked when Florence answered the phone.

"I'll say. She's taking him out of the country!"

"Calm down, Florence, and tell me what happened."

"Well, I was dusting downstairs when I heard them talking in the den. Sandra was going on about Nova Scotia, how they got 'the best granite in the world.' So he says, 'Let's go there.' This got her all upset. She said it'd ruin her reputation if Pastor Chittick found out. I swear, listening to that dame is enough to gag a maggot."

"Go on," Edith said. "What did Mr. Smithwick say to that?"

"He goes, 'Would you feel better if it was our wedding trip?'"

Edith sank into a chair. "I feared something like this."

"Listen, tomorrow I'm cleaning for Mrs. Wigglesworth. Should I say something to her? Her husband, rest his soul, was Mr. Smithwick's best friend."

"I don't know. She might think we've been eavesdropping."

"I'd never do that," Florence said, indignant. "Yet it kills me to stand aside and do nothing. Can't Mr. Smithwick see through that phony?"

"Apparently he's besotted by her."

"His wife must be spinning in her grave."

Thus Edith was not terribly surprised when Mr. Smithwick took her aside the following week to break the news: " . . . a simple ceremony and reception here, mostly people from the church . . ."

"Don't worry, Mr. Smithwick, I'll plan a special menu."

"Nothing elaborate. We want to keep it low-key."

"Certainly. Will your son be attending?"

"I've decided to tell him after the wedding. It was Ms. Flint's sugges-tion. Elliott is so far away and he'd feel obligated to attend."

"On the other hand–"

"After we return I'll write him. He'll appreciate knowing I spent my honeymoon in Nova Scotia, locating material for his mother's memorial bench."

"I'm sure you know best, sir."

"Which one comes with the little pancakes," Edith asked her nephew. "Moo Goo or Moo Shi?"

"Moo Shi," Roland said from behind his menu.

"That's what I'm ordering." She put her menu aside. "You look a little tired, dear."

"I'm training a new secretary, and before you ask, she's married with three children."

"It never occurred to me to ask, dear. I'm much too anxious to hear the results of your police friend's report on Sandra Flint."

"When I asked him to look into her background, I figured it wouldn't amount to more than a few parking tickets." He reached into his breast pocket and removed a folded sheet of paper. "I was wrong."

"Does that mean she's got a criminal record?"

"Not exactly, though her last two husbands died under questionable circumstances. Although Sandra wasn't a suspect, the police asked her to stick around. Nonetheless, in both instances she left town."

"Husbands? How many does she have?"

"Let me read the report." Roland slipped on a pair of glasses and read:

"In 1990, Sandra married Lawrence Smedlie, a wealthy 77 year old wid-ower from Wilsonville, Nebraska. Soon after, the couple were vacationing at a lakeside villa in Arizona. One day, late afternoon, the Smedlies were in a paddle boat in the middle of the lake when the boat capsized, throwing them into the water. Mr. Smedlie drowned.

"When police questioned the other vacationers, they claimed they'd heard a lone man shouting. Sandra said it was her husband, shouting for help. What's interesting is the fact that Mr. Smedlie's two adult children later brought a wrongful death claim against their father's widow."

"Good for them," Edith said.

"Sandra, however, was exonerated for lack of evidence."

"Of course," Edith said. "I imagine she's very clever."

Roland continued. "In 1998, she married Chester Huddleston, 80 years old, from Steubenville, Ohio. Mr. Huddleston had only been widowed eight months when he married Sandra. He died on their honeymoon in St. Croix."

"On the honeymoon? Dear God, what happened?"

"Apparently Mr. Huddleston had planned to scatter his late wife's ashes from a cliff. The couple had often vacationed on the island–"

"Don't tell me." Edith closed her eyes.

"According to the police report, while attempting to open the urn Mr. Huddleston lost his balance and fell to his death."

"No witnesses?"

"Just his bride, Sandra, who left the island soon after being questioned."

Edith gave him a baleful look. "That's where she's taking Mr. Smithwick–to the cliffs, to the granite cliffs of Nova Scotia . . ."

Three weeks later, Edith was arranging shrimp puffs on a platter when Florence, wearing a starched white blouse and tie, burst into the kitchen. "Mrs. Wigglesworth wants a glass of sherry."

"The ceremony starts in forty minutes," Edith said. "If we serve one, they'll all want some."

"Mrs. Wigglesworth always has a morning sherry," Florence said.

"Fine, but don't tell the others. How many people are out there?"

"About a dozen. Pastor Chittick's upstairs helping Mr. Smithwick with those things men put in their collars."

"Stays. Why doesn't the bride help him? She's right down the hall."

"Don't you know it's bad luck for the groom to see the bride before the ceremony?"

"Oh good grief," Edith said. Before she could comment further, a loud rapping sounded at the service door. "Get that, will you Florence? It's probably the ice delivery."

Seconds later Florence rushed back to the kitchen. "It's a policeman," she said in a hoarse whisper, "and he wants to speak to Sandra."

"Did you tell him she's about to get married?"

She shook her head. "I got too flustered when he flashed his badge."

"Very well then. Take him up the back stairs and point out which one's her room. And don't mention it to anybody. We don't want to upset Mr. Smithwick on his wedding day."

Minutes later Florence returned. "I did like you said. What do you suppose it's all about?"

"I have no idea," Edith said, "but we've got twenty guests to care for, so get out there."

When Florence left the kitchen, Edith turned to stare at the door leading to the stairs. Before long she heard clattering footsteps followed by the slamming of the service door. She took off her apron, hanging it on a hook in the pantry. Then she opened the door and slowly climbed the narrow back stairs.

At the top, she stopped to catch her breath. It was quiet upstairs. Midway down the corridor, a bedroom door was open. She approached and peered inside. The room was in chaos: dry cleaner bags, panty hose, clothing tags and coat hangers lay tangled on the bed. Strewn across the bureau were hair curlers, cosmetic bottles and tissues. She studied the message written in lipstick on the mirror: *Angus, I'm sorry, Sandra.*

At least she's got the decency to apologize, Edith thought, closing the door behind her. She went downstairs, moving through the kitchen to the living room filled with elderly guests talking loudly. Two young women from the church, hired for the occasion, served tea from a big silver pot.

Pastor Chittick dozed in a wingback chair. Edith gently shook his arm. "Pastor, where's Mr. Smithwick?"

"What? He's still upstairs in his room." He squinted at his watch. "I suppose we should get him down here."

"Wait a moment, will you?" She scanned the room, finally spotting Mrs. Wigglesworth. The elderly lady was perched on the piano bench, happily sipping sherry. Edith took her aside and quickly filled her in on the latest development.

The woman didn't seem surprised. "That gal did Angus a favor," she said. "You want me to break the news to him?"

"If you would," Edith said. "You've known him longer than anyone."

"More than fifty years," she said, swaying slightly. "Let me talk to the old fool."

Edith watched the woman climb the stairs. Then she rushed into the kitchen and pulled bottles of champagne from the refrigerator. While she was opening them, Florence appeared.

"Why are you opening the champagne now? Won't it go flat?"

Edith filled her in on the bride's hasty retreat.

"She's flown the coop? That cop must have put the fear of God in her. I wish I knew what he said."

"We'll discuss it later," Edith said, handing her a champagne bottle and two glasses. "Take this upstairs to Mr. Smithwick's room. I have a feeling he can use it right now."

Florence stared at her. "You mean you're not calling the party off?"

"I've got three dozen crab puffs, two gallons of lobster bisque and enough salmon mousse for the entire church. It will not go to waste."

"But—"

"Just fill their glasses and say there's been a change in plans."

"You're the boss," Florence said with a shrug.

Later, when Florence returned, Edith was in the process of cutting the wedding cake. "Look," Florence pointed out, "the little bride and groom are missing from the top."

"I removed them," Edith said, "under the circumstances."

"You saving them for someone?" Florence asked, nudging Edith.

"Yes, for my nephew Roland. One never knows."

"I'd like to meet him sometime," Florence said. "He got the goods on that dame."

"Maybe you will," Edith said.

There was no need to tell Florence she'd already met Roland earlier when he appeared at the back door and flashed his badge. Initially her nephew had refused to go along with Edith's plan: impersonating a cop. But Edith had talked him into it. She knew that the sight of a badge would so completely unhinge Sandra Flint that she wouldn't realize the badge read: *Campus Safety.*

Now she handed Florence a knife. "Don't just stand there. Help me cut the cake. We've got guests to feed."

"Whatever you say, boss."

"MURDER AT THE SENIOR CENTER"

Nadine always arrived early at the Brightside Senior Center to make sure everything was in place: coffee pot plugged in, doughnuts stacked on serving platters, sugar bowls and creamers filled. As she drove into the parking lot, she noted Frank's maroon Taurus once again blocking the rear door. Thus when she attempted to access the stairs, her coat caught on the car's dusty grill. To make matters worse, he'd left the back door unlocked.

No doubt Frank had punched in and immediately headed to the corner diner for coffee and gossip. One morning while the center was unattended, someone sneaked in and stole the presents under the tree. The thief must have been disappointed with the loot. The gifts consisted of deodorant, shampoo and foot powder, all intended for a local nursing home.

In the chilly kitchen Nadine filled the milk pitchers. Carrying a tray of donuts, she noticed the plastic covering had been carelessly rewrapped. Two donuts were missing. She sighed. Granted they were day-old donuts, selling for 25 cents. Nonetheless, the money bought items for the holiday raffle baskets. Not only that, Frank could afford to pay. A long-time city custodian, his paycheck was undoubtedly larger than Nadine's activity director's.

After plugging in the big aluminum coffee pot, she arranged silverware in the rear of the cafeteria. *Let it go,* she reminded herself, ripping into a package of napkins. Complaining did little good. Sheila, the center's executive director, liked Frank. He called her "boss lady" when fetching her morning coffee and pastry.

As Nadine centered paper doilies on serving platters, an unsettling thought arose: Yesterday she'd hidden a half dozen ice cream sundaes in the big freezer. The treats were intended for Wednesday's Memoir Writing group. Each participant's $8 fee included the workshop, supplies, and a sundae.

Frank wouldn't, would he?

Nadine wiped her hands and marched into the kitchen, stopping at the waist high freezer. Flinging open the metal cover, she heaved aside bags of frozen French fries. She breathed a sigh of relief upon uncovering the hidden cache of sundaes. Then she gasped at what lay beneath: the frozen blue face of Sheila Krawchuck, Executive Director of the Brightside Senior Center.

"And did I mention the monthly department heads meeting?" Mrs. Verga, the mayor's executive assistant, handed Nadine a printed sheet.

Nadine wearily stuck it inside a thick folder on her lap. "Actually, Mrs. Verga, my job involved coordinating activities. I know nothing about running the senior center."

"The mayor knows that," she said. "He just needs an interim director. It's temporary, until a replacement can be found."

"I suppose I could handle it for a month," Nadine said.

"You're not afraid, are you? The mayor's promised increased security."

"Have the police gotten any leads?"

"They're focusing on the shelter down the street. We understand one of its residents broke in and stole Christmas presents from under your tree."

"He didn't actually break in," Nadine said. "The door was open." She resisted the impulse to mention Frank's carelessness.

"Unfortunately, you're not in the best location," the woman said. "I suppose you know that Sheila was mugged in the parking lot two weeks ago. The DPW immediately installed new lighting."

"I noticed the new lights," Nadine said. "I wasn't aware of a mugging."

"I imagine Sheila didn't want the members getting upset."

What about the staff? Nadine thought. "Did she identify the mugger?"

"The police have a description. They think whoever strangled Sheila was most likely a drug addict looking for money." She frowned. "Yet the doors were apparently locked that night with no sign of forced entry. The custodian claims he locked both front and back before leaving."

Frank must have been eager to punch out, Nadine thought, once again remaining silent. Despite the man's poor work ethic, he knew everything about running the center, from jump-starting its ancient furnace to ordering bathroom supplies. Furthermore, Frank's male presence would help ease the members' fears. She got to her feet. "I've got to get ready for tomorrow's reopening."

"The mayor's promised a police officer at the door," Mrs. Verga said, "though you'll probably only get a handful of members."

"I'm not so sure," Nadine said. "They hate to miss their Bingo."

Her words were prophetic. The members returned in droves, including some she hadn't seen in months. June, the center's art teacher, attributed this to morbid curiosity. "They don't want to miss the gory details," she told Nadine over coffee in the second floor art room.

"I just want the murder solved and a new director chosen so I can go back to being another cog in the wheel," Nadine admitted.

"At least you're a hands-on director. Sheila was always barricaded in her office," June said, "not to be disturbed."

Nadine nodded. "Sheila was the queen bee and we were the drones."

Though they were alone, June looked around before speaking. "I heard rumors that someone was buzzing around her hive."

"Do you mean that paper goods salesman? They spent a lot of time peering over his catalogs."

"I heard it was someone from the planning department," June whispered. "Things got hot and heavy. Apparently Sheila's husband got wind of it."

"Be that as it may, Sheila always balanced the budget," Nadine said. "You can't deny that."

"She was a multi-tasker."

Later that week, Frank set a cup of coffee on Nadine's desk. "My treat, boss lady."

"Thanks," Nadine said, noting it was from the kitchen and not the imported brew he'd bought Sheila. Nadine's reign, after all, was temporary.

During lunch she visited the cafeteria, where every table was filled. As she stood in line, a loud voice rang out: "Yoo hoo, Nadine!" She turned and spotted Mrs. Pemberton waving her napkin. The elderly lady shared a corner table with Lois, her hired companion.

"Sit," Mrs. Pemberton ordered when Nadine approached. "Lunch is dreadful as always, but we haven't talked in ages."

"I don't see a chair," Nadine said, surveying the room. She spotted Frank heading for the exit, his plate piled high.

Mrs. Pemberton spotted him too, and called out in a booming voice: "Excuse me, we need a chair!"

"I'm on my break," Frank called, flashing a grin and ducking out the door.

She waved him away. "That one's on a permanent break if you ask me."

"I'll find a chair," Lois said, getting up despite Nadine's protests. Minutes later she returned.

"Thanks. Looks like you found the last one," Nadine said. Turning to Mrs. Pemberton, she asked, "Are you staying on for Bingo?"

"Try keeping her away," Lois piped up.

Mrs. Pemberton laughed. "I'm afraid Bingo's become a passion. As my late husband Colonel Pemberton used to say, 'Please yourself and hell with the critics.'" Her voice quavered with age, her hands, with many ornate rings, trembled with palsy. During Bingo, Lois was needed to place the plastic chips on the numbers that Mrs. Pemberton indicated.

Now Nadine glanced at the clock. "Almost time to set up for Bingo."

"You're the director now," Mrs. Pemberton said. "Let someone else do it."

"Lately I'm wearing many hats," Nadine said.

"If they were smart, they'd hire you for the director's position."

"Thanks, but I'm not cut out for meetings and schmoozing."

Mrs. Pemberton raised a penciled eyebrow. "Your predecessor seemed to thrive on it."

When Nadine finally returned to her desk, she discovered a stack of mail piled high. As if she didn't have enough work to do, she had to handle the director's correspondence. Sighing, she dug in. Among the flyers and bills was a returned letter marked *Personal and Confidential*. The envelope, bearing the words *Return to Sender*, had obviously originated with Sheila. Judging by the stamps it had accrued, the letter had bounced around to three city departments before finally being returned.

Nadine turned it over. One reason for the confusion was because it was addressed to the city solicitor—the *former* city solicitor. He'd been fired after discussing Sheila's murder with a local reporter. Wisely, the new solicitor wasn't touching his predecessor's mail, Nadine thought, opening the letter.

It was dated three days before Sheila's death, a follow-up to a phone conversation she'd had. The subject was Frank. It read:

Here is the summary that you requested regarding Francis Masucci, custodian at the Brightside Senior Center: On two occasions in November, I witnessed Mr. Masucci taking money from the petty cash box kept in my desk drawer. The drawer is unlocked during the day and the average amount in the box is approximately $40. This money is used for incidentals: color photocopying, parking, tolls, etc.

When I confronted Mr. Masucci, he claimed he was using the money to buy birthday cards for our seniors. When I informed him that his actions would be documented, he protested, becoming angry. Please advise me concerning my next step in this matter.

Regards,

Sheila J. Krawchuck,

Executive Director

Nadine got up to stare out the window. When she'd made up her mind, she folded the letter, put it in her bag and got her coat. At the front desk, she told Alice the receptionist that she expected to be at city hall the rest of the afternoon.

The story made *The Brightside Banner* headlines: *"Custodian Questioned in Senior Center Murder."* The subheading read: *Police search house, find cash, checks.*

The following morning, Nadine found a half dozen TV news vans occupying the parking lot. Camera crews dragged cable lines across the asphalt. News anchors stood in front of the center giving live reports. She finally found a parking space behind the liquor store, closed at that hour. As she approached the center's front door, she was ambushed by a reporter with a camera man in tow. "Did the janitor kill Sheila Krawchuck?" she shouted at Nadine, thrusting a microphone in her face.

"Please, let me through," Nadine tried to turn away.

A young cop positioned outside stepped forward, unlocking the door to let her in. Undaunted, the reporter pounded on the glass to get Nadine's attention. Inside, Nadine raced up the stairs to the art room. She found June calmly placing jars filled with brushes on the long table.

"What a mob! How'd you get in?" Nadine asked.

"I pretended I didn't speak English," June said. She motioned to the coffee pot in the corner. "Looks like you could use a cup."

"Thanks." Nadine stopped at the window. Outside, the police officer was directing the news vans out of the parking lot. "Thank God they're leaving."

"Reading about Frank was depressing," June said, handing her a cup. "Granted he's got problems, but he's no murderer."

Nadine nodded. "As a thief, he's definitely small time. Still, you never know about people."

"What don't you know?"

The loud voice echoed in the high-ceilinged room. They turned to see Mrs. Pemberton in the doorway, leaning on her cane, with Lois at her elbow. The elderly woman wore an ancient fur coat with a purple scarf gathered at her neck.

"Mrs. Pemberton, how did you manage to get in?" Nadine asked.

"The credit goes to Lois. She was magnificent, flailing away at those horrible people."

"I was afraid they'd knock Mrs. Pemberton down," Lois said, blushing, "It's the police who deserve credit."

"We need their presence more than ever," Nadine said.

"Personally, I feel much safer with that dreadful man locked up," Mrs. Pemberton said. "I knew he was a bad apple just looking at him."

"Remember, Frank hasn't been charged with anything," Nadine reminded her.

"The police know he's the killer," the old lady said. "After all, they got a search warrant. You need proof to get one of those. Apparently some-one tipped them off."

Nadine wanted to change the subject. She'd told no one about Sheila's letter and how she'd turned it over to the mayor, who'd contacted the authorities. Maintaining a silence was difficult, especially as she'd gotten in the habit of sharing confidences with June.

Mrs. Pemberton sighed. "I suppose Frank's squandered the center's bazaar money. No doubt he's a gambler as well as a murderer."

"The police found some small bills and inexpensive jewelry," Nadine said. "The bazaar proceeds didn't amount to much."

"Didn't amount to much?" Mrs. Pemberton's voice broke. "What about my precious ring, the Star of Samoa?" She lurched forward, teeter-ing on wobbly legs.

Lois rushed to take the agitated woman's arm and lead her to a chair. "I'll get some water," she said, rushing from the room.

Nadine knelt by her side, taking the woman's hand. "Mrs. Pemberton, what is the Star of Samoa?"

"It's a ring that Colonel Pemberton got in the Pacific during the war. It once belonged to a nineteenth century Samoan queen. If you stand in the moonlight and gaze into it, you'll see a beautiful star."

"And you donated it to the bazaar?" Nadine glanced at June, who rolled her eyes.

Mrs. Pemberton nodded. "I wanted to help the center."

"Did you know about the ring?" Nadine asked Lois, who returned and handed her employer a Styrofoam cup.

She shrugged. "I'm afraid Mrs. Pemberton is very determined once her mind's made up."

The elderly lady struggled to sit up. "I wanted to raise money for the music room here. That ghastly old piano is horrible. I turn off my hearing aid during sing-alongs."

"Who did you give the ring to?" Nadine asked.

"Sheila, of course. She said she'd get it appraised."

"I promise to look into this, Mrs. Pemberton," Nadine said, rising. "Why don't you stay here and rest for a while."

At the door, June lowered her voice and asked, "Do you think Frank stole the ring?"

"He certainly had access," Nadine said. "On the other hand, a dozen people may have overheard Mrs. Pemberton talking about it. We assume it's valuable." She sighed. "I'll pass this information on to the mayor's office."

Downstairs, the lobby was abuzz with conversation. In the pool room, members stood around the table kibitzing, while in the card room the players ignored their hands in favor of gossip.

Nadine headed for the reception desk where Alice was deep in conversation with Yvonne and Florence, two regulars. They turned when she approached. "We're going to be on television," Florence said excitedly. "They filmed us getting out of our car."

"I hope you didn't talk to them," Nadine said.

"No, but I could tell plenty," Florence said. "How about the time Frank stole a frozen turkey from my car?"

"How do you know it was Frank?"

"It makes sense, now that we know the truth about him."

"Don't be too quick to judge," Nadine said. "And next time, lock your car." When they showed no sign of wandering away, she said, "Will you two excuse me while I talk to Alice?"

After they reluctantly left, Nadine asked the receptionist, "Do you know anything about a ring that Mrs. Pemberton donated to the bazaar?"

"I heard about it," she said. "Sheila locked it in her desk. She was going to get it appraised."

"Do you know if she did?"

"She never mentioned it, and the ring wasn't found."

"What about the bazaar? Do you have the figures?"

"Let me see." Alice opened a drawer and removed a folder which she flipped through. "Here it is. After expenses, coffee and paper goods, we took in $235." She ran a finger down the list. "The white elephant table, which included jewelry, made $48.75."

"Could the ring have inadvertently been sold?"

Alice shook her head. "I saw the jewelry. It was mostly inexpensive pins: owls and cats. The rings were the adjustable kind. I'm no expert, but nothing looked valuable." She put the folder away. "Talk to Dottie Biddle. She was in charge of white elephants."

"I will. In the meantime, I'll be at City Hall."

At the mayor's office, Nadine told Mrs. Verga about Mrs. Pemberton's ring.

"Oh dear, I'll take it up with the mayor when he returns from lunch," she said. "You've probably heard that Frank Masucci was released."

"Frank's out?"

"His alibi is airtight. The night Sheila died he was at his niece's Confirmation party. His lawyer provided videos of Frank singing Karaoke all night at the Legion hall."

"I never believed Frank was guilty," Nadine said. "Is he coming back to the center?"

She shook her head. "The mayor met with the DPW chief who agreed that Frank will work here at city hall, down in the archives."

Nadine sighed. "We could use some help at the center. The cafeteria floor and windows need washing."

"The DPW is sending someone next week. Part time is all the budget allows." She added, "You'll be pleased to know the trustees are setting up interviews for the executive director's position. Still, I wish you'd reconsider, Nadine. You've done an outstanding job as acting director under these circumstances."

Thank you, but I know my limitations." She got to her feet. "What should I tell Mrs. Pemberton?"

"Tell her the mayor's office is looking into it. In the meantime, I'll ask Sheila's husband to make a thorough search of their home." She paused. "Although he may not cooperate."

"Why is that?"

She glanced at Nadine. "I don't tell tales out of school, but it's no secret that Sheila and her husband were separated at the time of her death. He was renting a hotel room on Route 128."

"I'd heard stories as well," Nadine said. "Gossip is as popular as Bingo among the seniors." Indeed, with its cliques and petty jealousies, the center was much like high school . . . with dentures.

As instructed, Nadine documented her conversation with Mrs. Pemberton regarding the ring, sending the report to city hall via the inter-office mail. She also included a preliminary schedule of activities for January. Normally she'd have the programs already lined up, but the last three weeks had proved challenging. While the seniors were sympathetic, they nonetheless expected a full calendar of events for their $5 weekly dues. Two sing-alongs in one week was grounds for a riot.

Despite her intentions to leave work early, it was dark when Nadine locked the door behind her. The newly installed lights above the rear exit illuminated the adjacent parking area, leaving the back lot in shadow. She walked briskly to her car, noting the few vehicles remaining in the lot, most likely Christmas shoppers parking illegally.

A car slowly approached from the rear. As it moved closer, bright headlights flashed. Nadine shielded her eyes from the glare and walked faster. As she passed before the car, the engine roared as the car shot ahead. Nadine leaped and fell sprawling across the icy pavement. The car raced out of the lot, its tires screeching. She struggled to her feet in time to see it speed away.

In her glove compartment were antiseptic wipes which she dabbed at her raw, skinned knees, bleeding through the torn pantyhose. Unfortunately, they were a new pair; another reason she'd be happy to relinquish the director's position: no more pantyhose.

Thursday afternoon, Nadine visited the art room where a dozen of June's students milled around the long table discussing their paintings on display. "Got time for a cup of herbal tea?" June asked. "Chamomile helps you relax."

"Relaxation is not in my job description," Nadine said. "Right now I'm looking for Mrs. Pemberton. I've got good news." She spotted the woman at the end of the table, putting final touches on a painting. Lois sat nearby, looking on.

"That's very striking," Nadine said, studying the canvas. The runny watercolor looked as if it had been painted in the shower. "Listen, I've got good news. Will you be in tomorrow morning?"

"What's tomorrow?" the elderly lady asked Lois.

"Friday, and you've got Chair Yoga at 8:30."

"Perfect," Nadine said. "I've heard from city hall. Apparently Sheila's husband has found the ring. It was in an envelope with your name on it."

"Really? Oh, how grand. I suppose Sheila was waiting to get it appraised."

"Most likely," Nadine said. "It's being delivered sometime late this afternoon, and I'm locking it in my desk. You can have it tomorrow morning."

"You have no idea how relieved I am," she said, beaming.

Late that night, Nadine sat motionless behind her desk in the dark. She'd become familiar with the night sounds: the branch tapping against a window pane, the wall clock's steady hum, the periodic *whoosh* of air from the heating grate. Thus when she heard a soft scuff of footsteps on the stairs, she sat up straight and held her breath. When the steps reached the outside corridor she flicked on her flashlight, aiming the bright beam at the door.

"Shut it off!" The voice was harsh.

Nadine did as she was told. Then she reached for her desk lamp. *Click.* Nothing happened. "Did you cut the cables, Lois?" she said into the darkness.

"Alarms," the woman answered. "Can't be too careful. Now throw the flashlight over here and move away from your desk."

Nadine tossed it, saying, "Aren't you surprised, finding me here?"

"I don't surprise easily," Lois said, "although I was a bit shaken when Sheila walked in on me. She was hiding here, waiting to catch Frank in the act of stealing." She chuckled. "One thief trying to catch another."

"Why do you call Sheila a thief?" Nadine asked, keeping her voice calm.

"She stole my ring, the Star of Samoa."

"It's not your ring, Lois. And by the way, it's not here."

"It is my ring." The voice was a snarl. "The old lady promised it to me. She knew how much I loved it. Then she gave it to Sheila–for a goddamn piano." She laughed. "You really think Sheila was gonna turn the proceeds over to the center?"

"Lois, I said I had it in my office to call your bluff. I don't know where the ring is. Sheila may have been buried with it, for all we know."

"She wasn't. I checked during her wake. That meant one thing–the husband had it. I was waiting for him to move back into the family home." She chuckled. "You saved me a trip."

"What were you planning–breaking into the widower's house?"

In the dim light, the woman reach into her pocket and produce a ring of keys. "People are careless with these," she said. "Your friend June, especially. How do you think I got in here?"

"Lois, listen to me. I ran a CORI check on you. The police faxed the results yesterday. A whole page of crimes against the elderly. The cops are wise to you."

But she wasn't listening. "People like Mrs. Pemberton deserve whatever happens to them. They donate to charity, but the folks who put up with their crap day after day get nothing." She shifted her flashlight to Nadine's face. "Now give me the ring. Don't try to be a hero. I've got a black belt in tae kwon do." She produced a strip of cloth from her pocket and held it taut between her fists.

As she moved closer, Nadine shouted, "June!"

The door to the ladies room burst open. "Nadine!"

When Lois spun around at the sound of June's voice, Nadine rushed her. But Lois was quicker. In a flash her foot sliced through the air, connecting with Nadine's chin. Nadine staggered back, toppling over a chair. Stunned, she tasted blood in her mouth. As she struggled to her feet, June shouted, "She's getting away!"

Nadine grabbed the flashlight and raced out the door. At the top of the stairs the flashlight's beam illuminated Lois, flying down the steps with June far behind. As Lois reached the door, it suddenly swung open to reveal Frank, a coffee cup in his hand.

"Grab her!" June yelled.

Frank dropped the cup and lunged at Lois. Once again her foot shot out. But before it could make contact, she slipped in the spilled coffee and crashed to the floor. Frank pounced on her.

"You sit here, straddle her," he instructed June. "Nadine, sit on her legs while I get some duct tape." He vanished inside the maintenance room.

Nadine lowered herself onto Lois, who appeared dazed. As they held the woman down, the lights in the center went on.

June sighed. "Good old Frank."

"Would you prefer cream?" Mrs. Verga asked, holding the pot aloft.

"Milk's fine," Nadine said. She watched the woman pour coffee into china cups. "I'm curious to know what the new director's like."

"He seems . . . interesting," Mrs. Verga said. "He plays the cello and raises champion pugs."

"I'll be glad to hand over the reins," Nadine said.

"Oh yes, before I forget . . ." Mrs. Verga opened a desk drawer and removed an envelope, handing it to Nadine. "This is a bonus from the mayor. It's his way of saying thank you for keeping the center running while we found a new director. Not to mention your involvement in capturing Sheila's alleged killer." She glanced at Nadine. "My dear, you exposed yourself to great risk that night."

"I had backup."

"Do you mean June? What if Lois had had a weapon?"

"We thought of that, so June stashed a croquet mallet in one of the bathroom stalls."

"Oh. I didn't hear about that."

"That's because, uh, she forgot which stall."

Mrs. Verga shook her head. "All that for a ring that may never be found."

"You could be right," Nadine said. "Now I'd better go. There's lots to do before the new director arrives." She got to her feet. "Tell the mayor thanks. Ask him to go easy on Frank. If he hadn't shown up that night, Lois would have vanished."

"A letters of commendation will go in Mr. Masucci's file," she said.

"What puzzles me is how Frank got a key to the center," Nadine said. "We'd changed all the locks."

"Apparently he borrowed the key intended for your new custodian," she said. "Mr. Masucci is certainly resourceful, isn't he?"

"I never learned why he showed up that night," Nadine said.

"He wanted to clean out his locker. Had he shown up during regular hours, he felt he'd be turned away."

"Not by me," Nadine said. "A couple of missing donuts is nothing to get worked up about."

When she returned to her office at the senior center, the usual pile of mail awaited. Among the flyers, bills and brochures was a letter to Sheila Krawchuck, Executive Director, from the Brightside Savings Bank. Nadine opened it, determined to settle her predecessor's issues before the new director arrived. Inside was a notice informing Sheila that the one-month expiration date on her safe deposit box was approaching, and would she like to continue at the special rate?

Nadine smiled to herself as she scribbled a note to Mrs. Verga, which she attached to the bank's letter. She slipped both inside an envelope, addressing it to the mayor's office. It could take months before the legal issues were settled and the safe deposit box finally opened. When that moment arrived, Nadine had a very good idea what it might contain.

She went down the stairs, pausing to drop the letter in the inter-office mail box. From there she headed to the lounge.

Time to set up for Bingo.

"THE LOVE NEST"

The red Miata bounced over the frozen grooves in the narrow, snow-covered road. Vivienne turned the wipers on high, yet they couldn't compete with the heavy flakes tumbling from the sky. She wondered what she was doing on a deserted road in the middle of nowhere with a blizzard in progress. Why hadn't she insisted on driving to the cabin with Arnold? Why jeopardize her life because he was afraid of Lorna, his wife.

She groaned when the car lurched and the left rear wheel sank into a rut. Frantically, she pressed her foot on the accelerator only to hear the high-pitched whine of spinning tires. Flumes of snow shot into the air while the car nestled in deeper. She cursed and shut off the engine and fumbled in her bag for a cigarette.

After a few moments she lowered the window and glanced warily around. The towering evergreens lining the road shook in the wind, their boughs heavy with snow. Behind her, the road vanished in a screen of white. She was alone in the White Mountains, appropriately named, and her cell phone was useless. At least the cabin wasn't far away. She'd have to walk–and ruin her new suede boots.

Damn Arnold!

Before climbing out, she stuffed the Miata's keys under the visor. Since it was Arnold's fault she was stuck, he'd better find a towing service, one that would venture out in this weather. She stood up, zipped her short fox jacket and began trekking through snow in high-heeled boots.

Before long her feet were wet, her toes numb. Don't dwell on it, she told herself. Instead, think about the blazing wood stove and chilling wine inside the cozy cabin ahead. It was their love nest, as Arnold called it, a refuge where he felt safe from Lorna's prying eyes. She remembered his jubilant voice on the phone that morning. At first she'd assumed he was calling to cancel their weekend. After all, the weather stations were predicting a Northeaster. Nonetheless, Arnold was giddy: "Let it snow, baby. Lorna's leaving for Florida to think things over. This time, I'm sure she'll negotiate."

Vivienne yawned. She'd heard it all before. "How do you know?"

"I overheard her talking to the lawyer. He'll probably take everything I've got, but who cares when I can be with you."

"Not everything, I hope," Vivienne said sweetly.

Now she stopped to brush the flakes from her long dark hair. Through the swirling snow the faint outlines of the cabin appeared ahead. A ribbon of smoke rose in the sky. With a sigh of relief, she pushed onward.

Outside the cabin, the bulky form of Arnold's SUV lay hidden under a blanket of white. She followed a shoveled path nearly obliterated by drifts leading to the stairs. Climbing to the top, she paused on the deck to look out at the snow-covered lake. Pinpoints of light from a lone house on the opposite side twinkled in the winter dusk. The house looked homey, like a scene from a calendar.

She continued through knee-deep snow to the door. "Sweetie, I'm here," she called, stepping inside to the welcoming warmth of the wood stove. Soft jazz played on the stereo, and on the counter, a silver ice bucket held champagne.

"Arnold?" she called, slipping out of her damp jacket. No response. Most likely he was doing something silly and romantic, like hiding bottles of wine in the snow. Later they'd make a game of finding them. In any case, she was too exhausted to care. After kicking off the soggy boots, she collapsed on the sofa. Pulling a quilt over her, she fell into a deep sleep.

An hour later she woke to a weather report issuing from the stereo. It was interspersed with static–warning of gale force winds. She sat up and groped for her cigarettes in the dim light. The cabin was cold; the fire had died in the wood stove. She shivered and looked around the shadowy room.

Where was Arnold?

Wrapping the quilt around her, she moved to the sliding glass doors and peered out. Snow drifts ringed the lake, surrounding the dark ice. Was it solid this time of year? Had Arnold attempted to cross it? She dragged on her cigarette, remembering something else: the bear tracks they'd spotted last fall. She shook her head. Her imagination was running away with her. Arnold's absence most likely involved Lorna. No doubt she'd called with some desperate excuse–an accident or make-believe illness. The SUV battery was probably dead so he'd taken a cab into town and rented a car. Knowing Arnold, he'd been in a dither and forgot to leave a note.

She nodded to herself. Yes, of course Lorna was behind Arnold's absence. The woman was a classic manipulator and he was Play-doh in her hands. Vivienne pursed her lips. She felt no pity for Arnold's wife, who owned a townhouse in Boca Raton, filled with her golf trophies. Not only that, she'd had 30 years with Arnold. It was time to step down to make room for Vivienne.

Hasta la vista, Lorna.

She shivered, pulling the quilt closer. No matter what time Arnold returned, the stove needed wood or she'd freeze to death. She sat and reluctantly pulled on the damp boots. When she tugged open the sliding glass door, snow tumbled inside.

She trudged through knee-high drifts to reach the wood pile at the end of the deck. Its blue plastic covering was heavy with snow. She grabbed the corners with both hands and yanked it off. Underneath the pile of neatly stacked logs, Arnold lay stiffly on top. Dark blood had congealed around a deep wound in the center of his forehead. His eyes, always so adoring, now regarded Vivienne with indifference.

She screamed and covered her mouth. Then she stopped and turned, her eyes darting everywhere. The trees surrounding the cabin were as dense as a fortress, their branches creaking in the wind. A blue-white moon above cast eerie purple shadows on the snow drifts, creating an alien landscape. The wind howled an anguished lament as she peered into the darkness . . .

Hours later, she huddled near the wood stove, clutching a metal poker. Her eyes strayed to the sliding door. The wind shook the glass and shrieked down the stovepipe. Each new sound made her jump. She needed cigarettes; she'd smoked her last, yet knew where to find more: Arnold kept extra packs of her brand in the SUV's glove compartment.

Dare she venture out? As she contemplated the idea, a cinder popped and she shrieked, her heart racing. It was no use—she needed cigarettes.

Once again she pulled on the boots, now dried and stiffened, and wrapped the quilt around her. Outside, she grabbed a shovel and moved to the top of the stairs. The SUV below resembled a hulking beast under its coat of snow. Holding the quilt closed with one hand and the shovel with the other, Vivienne descended the steps.

Upon reaching the SUV, she dug around the driver's door until it swung free. She pulled herself up onto the seat, panting with exertion. Inside the vehicle her breath made clouds in the darkness. She fumbled for the interior lights, turning the switch. Nothing happened. Just as she had suspected, the SUV's battery was dead. At least there's cigarettes, she thought, reaching in the darkness for the glove compartment.

As she did, a hand clamped down on her arm and a voice flat and hollow said, "Hello, Vivienne."

She screamed and kicked the door open. After leaping into the snow, she scrambled to her feet and charged through the drifts. The cold cut like razors against her bare legs but she scarcely noticed in her desperation to get away. The lake was her only hope. If she could reach the opposite side and the house whose light cast its glow upon the ice . . . .

She trudged downward, finally reaching the lake. A cold wetness seeped into her boots as she slid across the ice. She glanced over her shoulder. A dark figure struggled down the hill, steadfastly following in her footsteps. Vivienne moved further onto the ice. It was wet but sturdy underfoot. She broke into a run. The wind tore at her clothes and tears froze on her face.

When she was halfway across, the rumbling began. Although the sound was muted by the the wind, she felt the vibrations. The early winter ice was thrumming an erratic rhythm whose chords radiated across the lake. She ran faster, her breath ragged.

The first crack tore the air like a lightening bolt. The ice buckled and bucked, coming apart with a great rending. Vivienne fell to her knees. When she got up, another crevice appeared. She leaped over it and watched in sick fascination as it widened. When a crack appeared underneath her, it was too late.

She fell backwards into the inky water, her sodden fox jacket a dead weight. Water poured into her nose and throat as she tried to scream.

Before long she ceased thrashing . . . .

Back on the shore, Lorna stood and watched. When all movement on the lake had ceased, she turned and retraced her steps up the hill. The quilt lay on the ground next to the SUV. *How convenient,* she thought, carrying it to the cabin's deck where she spread it out at the base of the wood pile.

The next step was tricky: lifting her husband's body without creating a log slide. She braced her back and flexed her knees, a familiar golfer's stance. In one smooth motion she lowered the body to the quilt. For a moment she gazed upon her husband's frozen face and felt no remorse. "Betrayer," she whispered, rolling the quilt around him. Then she dragged the body across the yard to the SUV. The snow provided a smooth passage. Finally, she hoisted the unwieldy bundle into the back seat and slammed the door.

Now she stopped to rest. The wind had died and the moon cast a silver sheen over the lake. On the opposite side, the lights from her cabin glowed. She'd grown to cherish her little hideaway. After learning about her husband's love nest, she'd rented the cabin because the view was excellent. During the summer, she spent many hours observing the love birds through binoculars. She watched them cavorting, naked as slugs, on their deck. From across the lake she'd listened to their lewd laughter.

Finally, she went inside. Going from room to room, she tossed everything into a plastic trash bag. In the kitchen, she spotted the champagne on the counter. Arnold had been in the process of opening it when Lorna had arrived, surprising him. She'd announced why she was there: for a chance to talk before she left for Florida. One last opportunity to hear him admit he was ending their marriage of 30 years. It had been a good marriage–until Vivienne had slithered into the picture.

Naturally Arnold was shocked to see Lorna at the door of his love nest. Nonetheless, he'd said little as she attempted to talk sense into him. As she pleaded, he'd worked the cork from the champagne bottle. After her speech, he'd turned his back to her. She'd dashed out, humiliated, to her car.

It was while driving back on the snow banked road that the thought took hold in her mind: her husband had been opening a bottle of Dom Perignon Champagne. *Dom Perignon!* Throughout their marriage–the anniversaries, birthdays, even when she won the Women's PGA Championship–he'd never bought Dom Perignon. Granted, she wasn't the type who demanded luxuries. In fact, her practical nature had once appealed to him.

Thus her thoughts had swirled like the snow falling around her, yet at the same time she felt strangely removed. When she'd driven halfway down the road, she stopped abruptly. As if powered by remote control, she got out and opened the trunk. From her golf bag she removed a six iron. She got back in the car and reversed her direction.

This time when her husband opened the door, it was she who was silent.

Now the ice clung like barnacles to the SUV's windshield. Lorna attacked it with a plastic scraper, eventually clearing a tiny area. She tossed the trash bag and its contents into the back seat next to the quilt-wrapped body and climbed behind the wheel of the SUV. When the engine roared to life, she drove the few yards to the crest of the little hill that ran down to the lake.

The car sat poised at the top. Lorna smiled with satisfaction as she pictured the SUV gathering speed as it rolled–much like a golf ball when the greens were fast. She shifted into neutral and held the door open with her foot. Before releasing the brake and leaping out, she spotted the blood-covered head of her golf club under the passenger seat.

Careless, she thought, stretching to retrieve it. As she did, a rogue wind, a remnant from the storm, swooped down and slammed the door shut. The impact jolted the SUV. It lurched and slowly lumbered down the hill, picking up speed on the icy run.

Inside, the SUV was dark; the ice-covered windshield offered no illumination. Lorna groped for the light switch, forgetting in her panic she'd disabled it earlier. When the car came to a sudden stop, she was thrown against the dashboard. Dazed, she sat up, fumbling for the door. The handle moved freely but the door wouldn't open. She butted it with her shoulder and then kicked at it with her heavy boots.

In desperation, she wrapped her hands around the golf club's rubber-coated grip and swung hard at the windshield. When the glass shattered, it wasn't cold night air that rushed in, but frigid lake water. She scrambled into the back seat to escape. Her husband's body, freed from its quilted shroud, lay sprawled across the seat. Twig-like fingers caught in her hair. She screamed. Meanwhile, the SUV's windows, reacting to the mounting pressure from outside, burst.

A river of arctic water poured in, silencing her.

The young man stood hunched at the side of the road, his thumb out to passing traffic. His face was partially hidden by the hood of his sweatshirt. He'd been standing there for half an hour. The few cars that passed hadn't even slowed. Maybe the drivers didn't like his torn jeans or long hair, he thought. People in the country judged harshly.

All he wanted was a ride, no questions asked. And though he'd do better on the main road, he couldn't risk it in case his mother had called the police.

He felt bad that things had ended like that, but sooner or later something was bound to happen. His drunken stepfather had hit him for the last time. He wasn't going back. He pulled his sleeve over his throbbing hand. Maybe it was broken. The old bastard had a jaw of steel.

When a gust tore at his thin clothing, he began walking fast. The wind was like his life—never cutting him a break. He eventually broke into a trot. Before long he came upon a narrow dirt lane. It was a former cow path, now a private road leading to the lake. Similar roads in the area existed for city people with summer homes rarely used in winter.

Thus he was surprised to see fresh tire tracks partially covered in snow. Why would someone drive up here in a blizzard? Maybe it was a break-in, he thought, his heart beating fast. He glanced around and seeing no one, ducked into the road. Probably it was nothing at all, but at least he'd be out of the wind.

He hadn't gone far when he spotted the snow-covered red Miata. Slowly he approached it and with his forearm, wiped the driver's window. The car was both unoccupied and unlocked. He lowered himself into the driver's seat and glanced around. It was a sweet little car whose owner was obviously a slob. Old coffee cups, used tissues and parking tickets littered the floor. When he lowered the visor, a set of keys fell into his lap. He laughed out loud when the first key he tried opened the glove compartment. Inside was a stack of credit cards. He shoved them in his pocket and put another key in the ignition, muttering a prayer. The engine roared to life; the fuel gauge indicated a half tank of gas.

Yet when he shifted into drive, the Miata didn't budge. He got out and examined the sunken back tire. It was wedged in, but if he rocked the little car . . . Soon the tire was free.

Back in the driver's seat, he shifted into reverse and backed up the length of the narrow road. When he reached the end, he sat there, the engine idling. Interstate 95 was two miles away. It would take him all the way to Florida. He knew from watching TV that Miami was the place to sell a car. With the money, he could start his own business repairing motorcycles. He was good with bikes.

He let out his breath. Maybe his guardian angel had taken pity on him. Maybe for once in his life he'd gotten a break. In any case, he wasn't going to hang around analyzing the situation.

When the road was clear, he swung the Miata into the street, shifted into drive and accelerated. Moments later he turned on the headlights as he approached the upcoming exit.

"DUAL BRIDES"

Sisters Stella and Nora were polar opposites. Stella was the practical one who saved the family's table scraps for the pigs. Nora was imaginative. She designed a swinging door that allowed entrance to the barn cats while keeping out the skunks. Despite their apparent differences, when it came to men the sisters were in accord. Both fell for handsome farmer Earl Klopotoski.

As a bachelor, Earl wasn't the most honorable of men. He never told Stella he was dating Nora, and vice versa. Thus it was no surprise when the sisters discovered they were pregnant. They fought between themselves over the feckless Earl. Finally, Grandpa Spinney stepped in and settled the matter: Earl would marry both sisters, he announced. Dual brides were not unknown in the valley, although the practice had fallen out of favor.

Not long after the wedding, Stella and Nora gave birth to sons. As the boys grew, the sisters grew closer. They learned to work together, pooling their skills to help run the farm. Stella drove the tractor and tended the crops. Nora schooled the children and made their clothing. Under the sisters' management, the farm prospered.

In fact, the farm did so well that Earl found himself with time on his hands. He began going into town after dark, "to play cards," he said. He'd come home late and stagger to the door. Most nights he ended up slumped over the steering wheel of his truck. Stella, the stronger of the two, would get out of bed to drag Earl into the house.

"He's romancing the new waitress," she confided to Nora one day. "I overheard them talking at the grain store."

"So that's where our money is going," Nora said. "He claimed the cows haven't been milking."

"They've been milking fine. It's Earl who's lost his head."

"What do we do?" Nora picked nervously at the fabric of her apron.

"We hope he comes to his senses," Stella said. "But it's not likely, the way he's drinking."

The arrival of winter didn't slow Earl down. In fact, it became an excuse to stop work early and head into town. One snowy night, after the children were tucked into bed, the sisters sat by the wood stove. Stella peeled potatoes while Nora worked on her embroidery. Outside, the wind rattled the panes.

"Go on up," Stella finally told her sister. "I'll wait for him."

Later, Nora was roused from a deep sleep. "Come quick," Stella whispered. Snow clung to her hair. "It's Earl."

Nora followed her sister through the drifts to their husband's truck. Inside, he lay slumped over the steering wheel, his face gray.

"Carbon monoxide poisoning," Doc Moss announced at the scene. "Probably backed into a drift and clogged the exhaust pipe. Passed right out."

"Didn't you hear his truck?" a distraught Nora asked her sister after Doc Moss had gone.

Stella shook her head. "The wind was so loud . . ."

The next day Stella offered to go into town to make funeral arrangements. Nora took over her sister's chores. When she emptied the garbage into the pig's trough, she found a whole potato inside the bucket. It was unlike her sister to throw out a perfectly good potato, Nora thought, and examined the spud.

When she sniffed the odor of diesel exhaust, she understood . . . .

"FAMILY PRIDE"

Margot Talbot plopped herself into the hairdresser's chair with a sigh. Right away she was draped in a thin, plastic cloak as Betty Ann asked, "What can I do for you today, Mrs. Talbot?"

The woman threw up her hands. "I cannot live with this outdated hairstyle another minute. I need a new look by six o'clock tonight."

"Big night with the hubby?"

"Hardly," she sniffed. "Tonight the Business Women's League is giving me an award: Entrepreneur of the Year." She sighed. "I'm expected to make a speech."

Betty Ann clicked her tongue. "Mrs. Talbot, it seems you're in the news every day for some award or another. Everything you touch turns to gold."

Margot closed her eyes as Betty Ann spritzed her hair with a spray bottle. "Not everything."

"I don't believe that. You're a real go-getter, that's what you are. Didn't I read that you bought that old apartment building near the bridge? Going condo, they claim."

Margot smiled at herself in the mirror. "I'm thinking about it."

"Then why so glum?"

Margot glanced around to see if anyone was within earshot. She leaned forward and said, "Are you familiar with Mrs. Pinkerton?"

"The old lady in the big house out on Farm Lane?" When Margot nodded, she said, "She used to come in regularly for a perm. Haven't seen her for a while, come to think of it."

"Good! The less I see of Eleanor Pinkerton, the better."

The intense expression on Margo's face startled Betty Ann. "I admit she's a bit crabby, but–"

"Crabby? Eleanor Pinkerton is a witch! Not only that, she's torturing me."

Betty Ann glanced warily at her client. "How can an old lady trouble a dynamo like you?"

"It's true. Eleanor Pinkerton and her husband destroyed my family twenty-five years ago."

"How did they do that?" Betty Ann snipped at the damp locks.

"It's a long story," she said, closing her eyes. "You see, my father was a brilliant inventor, ahead of his time. In order to finance his latest invention he'd taken out a loan, using our house as collateral. I was in high school then, about to graduate." She turned to gaze out the window. "I'd planned a picnic for my classmates . . . lunch served by the pond. Mother and I worked on the menu. The invitations had gone out and . . ."

"Yes?" Betty Ann prodded the woman, who seemed to have drifted away.

"And then one day I came home from school to find Mother crying. She told me that Father's project had encountered problems. Did I tell you he was ahead of his time? The people in this town were slow to recognize his genius. What happened was, the bank foreclosed on our house." Her voice broke. "It was horrible. We had to move out."

Betty Ann rolled Margot's fine hair in plastic curlers. "That's a darn shame, Mrs. Talbot."

"Later we found out that Eleanor Pinkerton and her husband had snatched up our house at the bank's auction. Meanwhile, my family was forced to move into an apartment downtown. We were devastated, going from a fourteen room house to a small, dark apartment. You have no idea."

"A shame," Betty Ann said, beginning a new row of curlers.

"Knowing how much the graduation picnic meant to me, Mother went to Mrs. Pinkerton. She pleaded with her to allow me to have the party at the house—just the one afternoon. Do you know what that evil woman said?"

"What?"

"She said it was out of the question. The landscapers would be working on the property. Poor Mother was humiliated."

"Doesn't Mrs. Pinkerton's grandson live at the house now?"

Margot's laugh was harsh. "That's her crazy nephew, Dwayne. He lives in the boathouse with the bugs and mice. Paying the old bat a hefty rent, no doubt."

"I heard he was in Viet Nam and came back a little 'off.'"

"More than a little, judging by the looks of him."

The hairdresser stepped back. "Come sit under the dryer, Mrs. Talbot. Bring a magazine if you'd like."

Before the hair dryer was lowered, Margot raised her eyes and said, "Believe me, this story is not over. I intend to get my house back."

"Oh, I'm sure you will, Mrs. Talbot," she said, plunking the dryer down over her head and turning up the heat. "I don't doubt it at all."

Later that afternoon, Margot Talbot stood in a long line at the post office. She had ten minutes to pick up her dry cleaning before the shop closed. What was holding up the line, she wondered. Craning her neck, she saw the cause of the delay: her nemesis, Mrs. Pinkerton. Leaning over the counter, the old woman harangued the clerk, asking, "Why can"t I send it fourth class?"

"Mrs. Pinkerton, fourth class is for books and periodicals," the exasperated clerk replied.

Margot stared daggers at Mrs. Pinkerton's back. The richest woman in town, yet always trying to save a penny.

Finally, the old woman finished her business. Leaning heavily on a cane, she headed toward the exit, passing the long line. When she was abreast of Margot, she reached out to touch Mrs. Pinkerton's sleeve.

"You remember me, Mrs. Pinkerton? Margot Talbot. I'm in real estate and spoke with you about your house." She pressed a business card into the old woman's hand.

Mrs. Pinkerton, her face a mass of wrinkles, frowned at the card. "I don't remember that. Where did you get the idea I'm interested in selling?"

Margot felt her cheeks flush. "It was a couple of years ago. In the meantime, in case you decide–"

Mrs. Pinkerton shoved the card back. "I've decided nothing. And if I did, you'd be the last person I'd call."

When someone in line giggled, Margot turned to glare.

After concluding her business at the counter, she went outside. Across the street, Mrs. Pinkerton was getting into a rusted Mercedes station wagon. Her nephew Dwayne, a long gray pony tail hanging down his back, helped her in. Before pulling into traffic, he flipped a cigarette butt out the window. It rolled to rest at Margot's feet. As they drove past, the car backfired, engulfing her in a black cloud of diesel exhaust. She coughed, shaking her fist at the retreating car.

"I'll get you," she muttered. The Pinkertons had destroyed her life thirty years ago. She'd been powerless then, but today she had the means to fight back, and she intended to do just that.

That evening, Margot and Arthur Talbot had cocktails in their living room overlooking the swimming pool. Margot restlessly paced the room, smoking, and stopping to rearrange the magazines on the coffee table.

Finally Arthur lowered his newspaper to ask his wife, "Is there something wrong, dear? You seem agitated."

Margot crushed her cigarette in the ash tray. "You're a lawyer, Arthur. Let me ask you a legal question."

Arthur blinked. "By all means."

"Suppose someone promised you something, yet they never came through on that promise. Are they legally liable in some way?"

"Was the promise put in writing?"

"No, it was verbal."

"And were there witnesses to this promise?"

"No . . . no one."

He picked up his newspaper and resumed reading. "Then my dear, you don't have a case."

Margot stared intently at her husband, or rather, his newspaper. *"Arthur!"*

He sighed and lowered the paper. "Margot, we've been over this subject before. I will not discuss Mrs. Pinkerton tonight."

"But you don't understand. It was two years ago that I had a civil conversation with her. I'd driven by the house. Seeing her outside, I stopped and nicely asked if she ever decided to sell, she would contact me first. It would be to her advantage, rather than using an outside realtor who'd take five percent of the selling price. Mrs. Pinkerton understood this and said she'd let me know."

Arthur nodded. "So what is your problem?"

"My problem is the old bat's forgotten. She must have dementia. Meanwhile, it's obvious she's at the point where she can't take care of the place. She must be eighty-five, for God sake."

"Mrs. Pinkerton has a right to live wherever she wants, Margot."

She jabbed a finger at him. "What about me, Arthur? I'm almost fifty years old. How much longer do I have to wait?"

"You'll wait until Mrs. Pinkerton is ready to move out of her house."

"Her house? That is my house, my homestead." She glared at her husband, who appeared to be shrinking in his chair. "I won't rest until the Pinkertons realize that."

She stomped out of the room. Arthur sat quietly until he heard the bedroom door slam. Then he picked up his newspaper and continued reading.

Late that night, Margot sat in her study finishing up paperwork. After turning off the computer, she glanced at the phone. Then she moved to the bookcase, found the local phone book and opened it. Her finger traveled down the column of names: Peckham, Pellegrini . . . Pinkerton.

She picked up the phone and punched in the number. After several rings, a querulous voice answered: "Hello?"

Margot hung up. She turned off the light and sat in the dark for a few moments, smiling to herself.

"Lean your head back into the sink, Mrs. Talbot."

Margot relaxed as the hairdresser's strong, soapy fingers massaged her scalp. "You don't know how good this feels, Betty Ann. You're a wizard."

"Nothing at all, Mrs. Talbot. Are you getting any more awards?"

Margot yawned. "There's some citation from the community college. I often employ their interns." She laughed. "Free labor. But all in all, it doesn't amount to much."

"It's an honor to be singled out."

"Honors don't pay, and time is money."

The hairdresser, who stood for eight hours a day, knew all about time and money, particularly its lack. She changed the subject. "Heard anything from Mrs. Pinkerton lately?"

Horizontal lines appeared on Mrs. Talbot's forehead. "I'm convinced that woman is playing games with me."

"Why is that?"

"She's pretending not to know me. She's hoping I'll make a bigger offer."

Betty Ann worked conditioner through Margot's dyed, brittle hair. "Are you going to offer?"

"I'll offer what it's worth and not a penny more. Lord knows the place is falling apart. My parents would roll over in their graves to see how those people have destroyed our home."

"Have you been inside?"

"No, just from a distance when I happen to pass by that way."

Margot didn't mention that she passed by that way often, usually at night when she couldn't sleep. One night she'd had more wine than usual and had driven halfway up the driveway. The headlights off, she'd sat in her car and gazed at the old homestead, remembering . . .

Another night she'd gotten bolder. Keeping her head down, she'd crept to a line of bordering shrubs to hide in the shadows. The house and the adjacent boat house were in darkness. The only sound was the night breeze rustling the trees. She crawled closer to finally hide behind an overgrown rhododendron. Reaching into the pocket of her black trench coat, she felt for the paper-covered rock on which she'd written: *Get out now.*

She'd sent it flying. The sound of shattering glass in the still night was both terrifying and exhilarating.

Now Betty Ann, attempting to soothe her said, "All things come to those who wait, Mrs. Talbot."

Margot didn't bother replying. She knew that waiting was for other people, the dull and ordinary. Margot Talbot was not one who waited.

Before going home, she swung into the parking lot of the Village Liquor Shoppe. Lately a drink or two before bedtime helped calm her. In fact, it worked better than the tranquilizers her doctor had pre-scribed.

As she reached for the door, it burst open. A grinning Dwayne Pinker-ton emerged, a case of beer carried on his shoulder. He looked like a vagrant with his long gray hair and dirty sheepskin vest. Leering at her, he said, "Afternoon, miz Talbot."

With a look of outrage, she scurried past him into the store. Not only did the man look like an animal, he smelled like one too.

Later, over a candlelight dinner, Margot mentioned the encounter to Arthur. "A person like that shouldn't be allowed in a village like Granite Cove. Years ago he'd be locked up."

"I feel sorry for Dwayne Pinkerton," he said. " It can't be easy living in that boat house–no heat, no electricity."

"It's more than he deserves. The first thing I'll do is tear it down and build a nice, modern cabana." She took a sip from her glass of Cabernet and waited for her husband's response. When he didn't reply, she took another sip and said, "I know you think it's foolish, Arthur, my wanting the house after so many years."

"I admit I don't understand why you, an astute businesswoman, would want a house that's so neglected. Especially with so many attractive properties on the market."

"What can I tell you? Ever since the Pinkertons forced my family out I've vowed to get our home back." She shrugged. "Call it family pride."

"I beg to correct you, dear. The Pinkertons didn't force your family out, the bank did. Your father had taken out a huge loan to finance his . . . invention, and couldn't make his mortgage payments."

"Daddy's idea was ingenious. It was the provincial New Englanders clinging to the old ways that ruined him."

Arthur chose his words carefully. "Installing electric heating rods under a driveway was an innovative idea. It was also an enormously expensive one, which your father didn't take into account."

"Are you aware that people in Beverly Hills have movie theaters in their homes? In fact, they're considered mandatory."

"That's Beverly Hills, dear. This is New England, and back in 1974 people either shoveled their driveways or paid a high school kid to do it. No one was willing to spend thousands just to melt snow."

Margot stood up and threw her napkin at the table. "Are you calling my father a fool? I'll have you know, Arthur, he was a brilliant man. Some day that patent will be worth millions. We'll see who has the last laugh."

She knocked her chair over while rushing from the table. Arthur sat quietly until he heard the bedroom door slam. Then he reached for the Cabernet and poured the remainder into his glass. No sense in wasting good wine.

Late that night Margot roamed the downstairs of her house, unable to sleep. In the kitchen, she picked up the wall phone and dialed the familiar number. When she heard the reedy, elderly voice she said, in a low, guttural tone, "Get out now."

On Thursday, Margot rapped loudly on the door of apartment number seven. She wrinkled her nose at the cooking smells wafting from a nearby window. The Santoros, an older couple, were ethnic.

When Mrs. Santoro opened the door and saw Margot, her eyes widened. "Mrs. Talbot, is something wrong? My husband mailed the rent check two days ago at the post office."

"Ms. Santoro, do you own the clothes line outside?"

"My Carlo put it up behind the hedge. No one can see it from the front."

"Perhaps you didn't notice the new rules I posted in this building. Rule number 10 is no clothes lines. We have coin dryers in the basement for that."

"I know, Mrs. Talbot, but I like to hang Carlo's tee shirts in the sun. They smell so nice and fresh, you know?" She stepped back. "Would you like to come in for a coffee?"

The woman's voice, the smells, had given Margot a headache. "Take it down or face the consequences," she said before turning and stomping off.

Driving home, her headache persisted. She hadn't slept well last night. She'd driven to the local convenience store to use the outdoor pay phone in case Mrs. Pinkerton had put a tracer on her line. Since Margot had begun the late night calls and visits, they'd taken a life of their own. She couldn't stop if she wanted to. If she deliberated, she had only to remember the Pinkertons' cruelty. Instead of entering Wellesley, as planned, Margot had been forced to attend a state college. There'd been no end to her family's humiliation.

That evening, Margot knocked on the door of her husband's study. Lately, he'd been spending a lot of time holed up in there. "Arthur, I have another legal question for you."

He raised his eyebrows and looked at her without speaking.

"I need to know the laws regarding eviction proceedings."

"May I ask who you're thinking of evicting?"

"An old Italian couple at my building are breaking the rules. You wouldn't believe the smell of garlic coming from their place. I'll have to have the apartment fumigated once they're gone."

Arthur shook his head. "Tenants are entitled to cook in their own homes, Margot."

"It's more than that. They're primitive. They hang their underwear outside." She approached his desk and smoothed his hair back, saying plaintively, "Seriously darling, they're lowering property values. Don't you want me to be successful?"

Arthur noted the dark circles under his wife's eyes that she'd tried concealing with makeup. He knew she went out at night on mysterious errands; he felt it had something to do with the Pinkertons.

"I can't help you with this one, Margot. It's just plain wrong."

She stepped away from him. "Then I'll have to hire a lawyer. Imagine my own husband refusing to help me."

"Suit yourself, my dear. You always do."

At midnight, Margot sat in the darkened living room finishing her drink. She debated whether to drive to her old homestead. She needed a good night's sleep, yet felt a strong urge to go. She had a hunch the old lady was rattled and on the verge of moving. Victory was close at hand.

She reached for her car keys.

Halfway up the driveway, she turned off the headlights and coasted to a spot under a row of evergreens. A full moon illuminated the house. It had never looked so beautiful. Silently she got out of the car and crept closer, while at the same time scanning the ground for a rock to throw. As she was reaching for one, loud, angry voices rang out.

She stopped and listened. The shrill voice sounded like Mrs. Pinkerton's. The other, low and raspy, was Dwayne. The quarrel continued for a minute and stopped abruptly. Seconds later a high-pitched, drawn-out wail rang out and ended in silence.

Margot, poised to flee, listened intently. The house was as still as an abandoned church. One minute later, when a light appeared inside, she ran, gasping for breath. Upon reaching her car she leaped inside, turning on the ignition with trembling hands. She roared away, zig-zagging down the dirt road and didn't slow down until she reached her house.

Later, lying in bed, Margot shivered, remembering the angry voices and the loud scream. What had happened back there? Would she ever find out?

She didn't have long to wait. On Thursday morning she stopped at the Village Cafe. After placing her order for a decaf with skim milk, she glanced down at a shelf of newspapers. The front page of the *Granite Cove Gazette* carried the headline: *"Prominent Citizen Dies in Fall."* She snatched the paper and hurried for the door.

Sitting in her car, she read the story. According to the newspaper account, Mrs. Pinkerton, 84, had died of a broken neck after falling down the stairs at her home. She was discovered by her nephew, Dwayne Pinkerton, who had heard a scream and found her. *"She'd get confused and wander the house at night,"* the distraught nephew claimed. The account concluded with a brief history of the Pinkertons' ancestry dating back to the Revolution.

Now Margot edged her car into traffic. Still shaken, she debated her next move. Obviously Dwayne was responsible for his aunt's death. She briefly considered confessing to Arthur, and quickly rejected the idea. Arthur, a lawyer, would tell her to go to the police. They in turn would ask what she was doing at the Pinkertons' house in the middle of the night.

In the meantime, it was best to lie low. She would put the matter out of her mind for now. After all, she hadn't actually seen anything . . . .

There were a half dozen cars in the funeral home parking lot the night of Eleanor Pinkerton's wake. As Margot entered the reception area, she spotted Dwayne Pinkerton sitting on a sofa and reading a newspaper. He'd left the dirty sheepskin vest at home in favor of a sports jacket whose sleeves exposed hairy wrists. Dwayne didn't bother standing when Margot approached. Instead, he leaned back and grinned. "Well now, if it ain't miz Talbot come calling. I didn't know you were friends with my aunt."

Margot ignored the sarcasm. "Dwayne, I'm very sorry about your loss. I just want you to know that when you're ready to do something about the house, I can help." She handed him a card. "Please call. I think we can do business together."

"I'm sure we can, miz Talbot. I'm sure we can."

Weeks passed and she heard nothing from Dwayne. One day, as she drove past the village liquor store, she spotted the rusted station wagon outside. On impulse, she drove in and parked. Soon Dwayne emerged, carrying two cases of beer. She rolled down her window. "Excuse me, Dwayne?"

He put the beer into the back of the wagon, slammed the door and approached. "Miz Talbot, looks like you and me are frequent shoppers here."

She attempted a smile. "I was just wondering if you've had a chance to think about my offer regarding your house."

He rested a forearm on her window and looked inside. Feeling his eyes on her legs, she tried not to cringe. "I've been meaning to call and let you know," he said. "Tell you the truth, I'm sick of this town. Bunch of hypocrites. I got a buddy in South Dakota wants me to go in on a bar with him. I've been thinking about it."

"That's a good idea," she said. "What you do is get three different appraisals from three licensed realtors. The selling price will be whatever they average out to."

He paused and smiled. "Miz Talbot, people say you're a real dynamo. Now I believe it."

She nodded. "I have a reputation to maintain."

Before turning away, he winked. "You'll hear from me."

The call came two weeks later as she was leaving her office for the day. She recognized the raspy voice. "It's me, Miz Talbot. I'm ready to talk business."

"Good. Did you get the estimates?"

"I'm all set."

"Fine, then. Would you like to come to my office tomorrow?"

"No, here. Right now."

"Now?" She laughed. "But I don't even know the price. And we'll need to draw up documents, a Purchase and Sale Agreement—"

He cut her off. "You better come now if you want first dibs. Otherwise I got another real estate lady who's interested."

"That's fine. I'll bring a couple of standard forms, an Intent to Purchase and—"

She didn't get a chance to finish. Dwayne had hung up the phone.

This time Margot drove the length of the driveway and parked in front of the house, next to the ancient station wagon. She grabbed her briefcase and got out, looking around. Dusk was settling over the grounds. From inside, lights glowed dully. Now that ownership was near, she looked upon the property with a critical eye. Although the neglect was obvious, she was eager to begin the restoration. A labor of love, she thought. Every coat of fresh paint would be a tribute to her parents.

But first, she must face the unpleasantness of dealing with Dwayne Pinkerton. She knocked loudly on the door, noting the peeling trim. She was about to knock again when Dwayne appeared, dressed in a camouflage vest and holding a can of beer. He glanced at her briefcase. "Miz Talbot, you're a fast worker."

"No sense in wasting time," she said, following him into the living room. Her spirits plummeted upon seeing the cracks on the walls and water stains spotting the ceiling. The rug under her feet was blackened with soot from the fireplace. She was reluctant to sit on the chair that Dwayne offered.

"Beer, miz Talbot?"

"No thanks." She sat gingerly on a corner of the cushion. "I have to drive."

He stretched out on a sagging couch. "Normally I'm not allowed in the big house. Auntie didn't trust me."

Margot cleared her throat. "I understand your father and Mrs. Pinkerton's husband were brothers."

"That's right. When my father was down and out, old Albert wouldn't loan him a cent. Didn't approve of my dad, the black sheep of the family." He took a long drink from the can, watching her.

"And yet you ended up living here."

"If you could call it living. As she got older, Auntie was afraid to be alone out here in the sticks. I got to sleep in the boat house in exchange for doing chores. Now and then she threw me a couple bucks for driving her around."

Margot leaned down to open her briefcase. "Shall we discuss the sale? Do you have the realtors' estimates?"

Dwayne got to his feet. "Speaking of the boathouse, do you want to see it? I fixed it up pretty good, put in insulation and heat. C'mon, I'll show you."

Margot forced a smile. "Why not?"

She followed him out a back door off the pantry. She shivered when something skittered past her foot in the dark. They walked through overgrown wet grass to the boathouse. The door creaked when he opened it.

"Lemme turn on a light," he said, producing a book of matches from his pocket. He lit an oil lamp next to a rumpled cot. Soon a weak light illuminated the shabby interior. "Over there's my wood stove. Comes in handy winter nights."

Margot glanced around. Cobwebs hung from the ceiling and the smell of mildew permeated the air. Seeing her wary glance, he said, "It looks much better in the daylight. A coat of paint and you'll have it looking like something in a magazine." He lowered himself onto the cot and reached underneath to drag out a six pack of beer held together with plastic rings. He removed a can. "Sure you don't want a beer, miz Talbot?" He flipped open the tab.

"No, I don't. Let's go back to the house. I'd like to go over the documents."

He took a long swallow. "In a minute." He looked around the room. "Like I was saying, the boathouse could look real nice. You could fix it up for rental property. I says to myself, it's like selling two houses for one."

"What did the appraisers say?" she asked. "I need to see the estimates."

"There are no appraisals. I don't like strangers nosing around." He winked at her. "That's why I called you to do business."

"I don't understand—"

"It's easy, miz Talbot. I want a million for the place. Simple as that."

She stared at him and laughed. "I assume you're joking, Dwayne, but if you're not, I've run out of patience. This house is falling apart. It should be razed. You'd be lucky to get $300,000."

He lit a cigarette and leaned back on the cot. "Well, I guess we won't be doing business together . . . a shame."

She turned to the door. "Let's discuss this tomorrow when you're sober."

He crumpled the beer can in his fist. "I'm sober now and I want a million. Guess what? You're gonna pay it."

"I don't have a million dollars."

"You've got that nice house out by the country club, and that place you're turning into condos. Mr. Talbot's got a busy office downtown." He grinned at her. "I've done a little digging, Margot."

The thought of Dwayne Pinkerton checking into her affairs was infuriating. "You're awfully brazen for someone who's committed murder."

His eyes narrowed. "Who are you calling a murderer?"

"All right, I didn't want to say anything, but you forced me to. I was here, outside, the night your aunt died. I heard you arguing with her and I heard her scream. You pushed her, didn't you, Dwayne?"

He merely shrugged at her accusation. "I overheard her talking to a lawyer. She was planning to leave this house to the historical society. Meanwhile, her next of kin who's been waiting on her hand and foot gets squat."

She put a finger to her lips. "This conversation will go no further than this room. I can promise you that."

Now it was his turn to laugh. "Bet your ass it won't." He moved from the cot to an adjacent chest of drawers. From the top he removed a manilla folder which he handed to her. "Speaking of your midnight visits . . ."

Inside were several 8" x 10" photos, taken at night. In the top picture, she recognized herself crouching by the rhododendron bush, her face startlingly white against the shadows. In the second, she was running down the driveway, her Saab visible in the background. Silently she flipped through the incriminating stack.

"I used a special nighttime lens," he said, looking over her shoulder. "Over in 'Nam I did reconnaissance work. Comes in handy." He reached into his pocket and withdrew a flat black cylinder. "Listen to this," he said, pressing the device.

Immediately her voice, deep and guttural, filled the room: "Get out! Get out now!"

He clicked it off. "The first few calls I traced to your house before you switched to a pay phone." He shook his head. "You'd make a lousy spy, miz Talbot." Before she could comment, he added, "I also have plaster casts of your tire tracks, not to mention your prints on the rock you threw. If that ain't enough, any handwriting expert could identify your writing."

Margot struggled to keep her voice steady. "Regardless of your so-called evidence, the police would never believe you. They'd laugh. I'm a pillar in this town while you're nothing but a crazy person."

He took the file from her hand. "You might be right, miz Talbot. But I know someone who'd be very interested in what I have to say. His name's Lenny Santoro. He's the editor of the city newspaper. Matter of fact, you know his parents. They're the ones you evicted from your fancy condo building."

"The Santoros? He's . . . he's their son?"

"Check it out. Poor folks had to move in with Lenny cuz they had no place to go." He grinned at her. "Just imagine: Margot Talbot, pillar of the town, kicks an old couple out on the street. Then she scares an 84 year old lady to death with phone calls, broken windows and midnight visits."

She took a step back. "You can't frighten me, Dwayne. You killed your aunt. No one would believe your stories."

He leaned against the bureau. "Maybe not, but something tells me you don't want to take that risk." When she didn't respond, he added, "Look at it this way: I take the million dollars and leave for South Dakota. You get to keep your reputation and the house." His eyes moved over her body. "Don't look so upset, Margot. You're getting what you wanted." He crossed the room to clamp a hand on her shoulder. "Now quit stalling and write up that deed."

She nodded, shuddering as his hand massaged her shoulder.

"Write it up nice, Margot." His voice was husky. "Your hair sure smells pretty . . ."

"THE GOLDEN YEARS"

"Arnold, wake up!" Martha Hennessey jiggled her husband's lounge chair, shaking him awake.

"God sake, Martha, you don't have to shout." He opened his eyes to see a deeply tanned young man in mirrored glasses standing over them. His tee shirt read: Iguana Tours.

"This fellow's selling tickets for a boat ride to see the island," Martha said. "I thought it might be fun."

"Maybe later in the week," Arnold said, waving the boy away.

After the young man left in search of worthier prey, Martha sank back in her beach chair. "It's always later with you, Arnold. At least on a boat trip I'd have a chance to meet other people."

Arnold didn't respond. His head throbbed and his mouth was as dry as the sand beneath his feet. How many rum punches had he downed? The minute his wife left to go souvenir shopping, he'd made a beeline for the hotel's thatched roof bar. There he met a group of young people on spring break. They'd welcomed Arnold as if he were a frat brother, and not someone old enough to be their dad. One member of the group, a dark-haired girl in a yellow bikini, seemed particularly interested in him. As he was telling her about his recent promotion to VP in charge of of investments, Martha appeared to drag him away.

Now his wife slathered lotion on her arms, stopping to squint at him. "You haven't forgotten our lunch date with the Zacks, have you?"

"No, I haven't forgotten." Inwardly he groaned. It happened on every vacation: Martha latched like a sea lamprey onto some unsuspecting couple. On this trip it was Stanley and Ruth Zack, whom she'd met while collecting shells.

"You'll like them, Arnold. They enjoy the same things we enjoy."

"And what might that be, dear?"

"Oh, you know . . . dining, travel, stimulating conversation."

Stimulating conversation? The last time they'd had what might be called a stimulating conversation was 35 years ago on their honeymoon. The subsequent decades found them with little to discuss, outside of updates on the grandchildren.

At 1:30 Martha rose. "It's time to meet the Zacks."

Arnold struggled to his feet and followed his wife's broad sunburned back up the stairs to the outdoor terrace. When she spotted her friends slumped under a patio umbrella like two placid sea mammals, she gave a loud cry and rushed to their table.

"Nice to meet you," Arnold muttered, following introductions. As he'd imagined, the Zacks were nondescript Midwesterners, bland and boring. They were nothing like his new friends, the young people from the bar. Arnold remembered how the dark-haired girl had leaned back in her chair, resting a slim, tanned foot on his bar stool. For a moment he felt such yearning he wanted to cry.

After drinks were ordered, Martha regaled them with stories of trips taken years ago with her parents. "Daddy always insisted on a deluxe suite." To Arnold, his wife's voice sounded like a braying donkey's. Had she always been so loud? Never a shrinking violet, Martha had become something of a bully, insisting that Arnold embrace her newfound interests. "We must cultivate lasting interests for our golden years," she insisted.

Golden years. To Arnold the words conjured up images of retirement communities: lectures, Scrabble and golf. In the forefront, he and Martha like oxen, forever yoked.

While Martha and Ruth chatted, Arnold glanced at Stanley. The man's beige mustache resembled a well-used toothbrush. "What kind of work do you do, Stanley?"

"Retired," he said. "I was with the government–weights and measures."

"Ah, weights and measures." Arnold said, nodding.

Martha, hearing this exchange, leaned forward. "Arnold is in banking."

"Banking, eh?" Stanley said.

"Vice president in charge of investments," Arnold said.

"I think men are more able where finances are involved," Ruth Zack piped up.

"And women are more able at spending it," Martha said, laughing loudly at her joke.

The waiter arrived with their tray of iced tea. Although Arnold had desperately wanted a rum punch, he hadn't wanted to be the sole drinker.

Martha scooped sugar into her glass. "Have you heard about the turtle farm on the island? I'm told they have an excellent gift shop and cafe. We don't want to miss that, do we, dear?" With that, she kicked Arnold's sunburned shins.

"Ouch!" he cried. "Certainly not."

"We could all go tomorrow," Martha said. "What do you think?"

"Sounds like fun," Ruth said, turning to her husband.

Stanley cleared his throat. "Actually, I was hoping to get in some fishing. The hotel concierge said the best grouper is found off Parrot Key." He looked at Arnold. "Arnie? You interested in joining me?"

Although Arnold had zero interest in fishing, the thought of visiting a turtle farm with Martha and Ruth was too painful to contemplate. He shrugged. "Sounds good."

"It will give you fellows a chance to get acquainted," Martha said, beaming at Arnold.

"Let's meet at 5:30 tomorrow morning in the lobby," Stanley said.

"Fine." Arnold managed a smile. He hated rising early while on vacation almost as much as he hated being called Arnie.

The next morning Stanley, decked out in shorts and a fisherman's cap, met a bleary-eyed Arnold. "I've reserved a Boston Whaler for us," he said. "It's perfect for these waters."

"Fine," said Arnold, who didn't know a Boston Whaler from the Queen Mary. The last time he'd gone fishing was with his stepfather. The two had cast their lines off the town bridge. His stepfather caught a monkfish, the ugliest, scariest thing Arnold had ever seen. For weeks he had nightmares about the creature's great gaping mouth and spiky teeth.

After they selected their gear at a nearby marina, Stanley refusing Arnold's offer of money, they settled into the boat. Arnold sat in the bow. The odor of petrol hung in the air as they headed away from the marina to open waters, the nimble boat soon skimming over a clear turquoise sea. After twenty minutes they slowed and Stanley cut the engine, saying, "This looks like a good spot."

Arnold watched him assembling their gear. "Can I help?"

In response, Stanley dragged a Styrofoam cooler from under his seat. He flipped it open, revealing cans of Red Stripe beer nestled on a bed of crushed ice. "Help yourself, Arnie."

Arnold marveled at the wondrous sight. "Thanks!" This time he didn't mind being called Arnie.

Time passed while they floated, their lines in the water, the boat rocking gently. Arnold's forearms tingled from the sun directly above them. Drowsy from beer, he yawned, raising his can in salute. "Gotta hand it to you, Stan. You know how to live."

Stanley smiled. "Fishing was my escape from the job."

"Right. You mentioned something about weights and measures."

"Weights and measures? That's just what I told people."

Arnold puzzled over the cryptic remark, though not for long. A sharp tug on his fishing line demanded his attention. He sat up as the pole jerked and pulled, taking on a life of its own. "Whoa!" he said, yanking back.

"Easy there," Stanley said, moving closer. In a calm, unhurried manner he proceeded to guide Arnold through the process of reeling in his catch. Before long a shiny, sand-colored fish broke the water's surface, flipping and whirling in the air.

Stanley, net in hand, scooped up the fish and eased it to the bottom of the boat where it thrashed wildly. Arnold moved to get out of the way. "Sit," Stanley said. "You'll capsize the boat." He reached into the tackle box and produced a rock the size of a fist. "Sorry, fella," he said, addressing the fish. One blow and it lay motionless. Stanley carefully placed the fish atop the ice.

Arnold exhaled. "Wow. You're a pro."

"It's all practice," Stanley said, wiping his hands on a towel. "You showed some skill yourself."

Arnold reached for a beer, careful not to touch the dead fish. He took a deep swallow. "By the way, what did you mean with that remark, Weights and measures was what you told people?'"

Stanley was silent for a long moment, gazing out at the horizon. "What I meant was, for 30 years I was technically employed in the Department of Weights and Measures. My paycheck was signed by the head of that department. I was listed on the masthead as assistant registrar. Nonetheless, my duties, some of the time, were quite . . . different."

"What do you mean?"

"Let's just say that occasionally I was on the road for the government."

Arnold shook his head. "If I didn't know better I'd think you were some kind of hit man."

Stanley shrugged and began wiping the floor of the boat. Arnold sipped his beer and watched him. The idea of Stanley Zack involved in nefarious government deeds was preposterous. He was the most benign of individuals.

Stanley spoke, interrupting his thoughts. "I know what you think: someone like me. Even my wife calls me 'steady Stanley.' But wouldn't it make sense to choose someone who looks like a million other men? Someone who blends in?"

Arnold laughed. "I've had too many beers. I'm beginning to take you seriously."

"My work was something I never discussed. Even Ruth was unaware. Outside of a handful of men, no one knew."

"Then why are you telling me?"

Stanley was silent for a moment. "Maybe because in a couple of days I go back to Ohio and you go back to Massachusetts." He shrugged. "I feel a kinship with you, Arnie. We're two men facing the twilight years."

Arnold didn't know what to feel. The idea of Stanley leading a clandestine life was ridiculous. The man was no doubt another post-midlife male desperate to add a bit of drama to his life. Yet he couldn't get the image of him killing the fish with one blow.

Stanley interrupted his reverie. "It's getting hot. How about lunch? There's a place up the coast that supposedly has the best grouper sandwiches on the island."

"Sounds good. This sun's brutal."

Before long they were skimming over the ocean's surface, heading to shore.

Upon reaching the dock, Stanley sprang into action, securing the lines. He held out a hand to Arnold, who almost slipped stepping off the boat. Together they headed up a wooden ramp to the waterside restaurant. Arnold held onto the rope railing, woozy from sun and beer. They passed the outside deck, noisy with tourists and mariachi music blaring from speakers.

Inside, they found a quiet table away from the bar. Arnold tossed his menu aside. "Let me get a couple rum punches from the bar."

"You go ahead," Stanley said. "I'm going to need my head to navigate that reef later."

"You sure?" But he was already headed to the bar. He'd spotted the young people from the hotel sitting on the opposite side, laughing and clowning. He grabbed a drink and approached them.

The guys hooted and slapped his back as if he was one of them. The dark-haired girl, wearing a bikini top and brief white shorts, swiveled in her chair and smiled up at him. A jewel in her navel twinkled in the light. Arnold couldn't tear his eyes away.

"We're having a beach party tonight, Arnold," she said, "at midnight."

"Sounds like fun." He didn't mention that he and Martha were usually in bed by 9:30.

"I'll be watching for you."

Arnold gave her a furtive wink. Before returning to his table, he ordered a round of drinks for his new friends.

When Arnold returned, Stanley was digging into his sandwich. Another sat on Arnold's plate, next to a fresh drink. "I ordered for you," Stanley said, "along with a rum punch. We can't stay long before the tide turns."

"Thanks," Arnold said. He glanced at the sandwich; he was no longer hungry. He picked up his drink.

"Friends of yours?" Stanley asked, gesturing to the laughing group at the bar.

"College students on spring break, staying at our hotel," Arnold said. "Nice bunch of kids."

"I suppose you'll be doing more traveling, now that you're retiring."

"Who said I was retiring?"

"Martha. She said next year."

"She's wrong. I have no intention of retiring." He wished Stanley would stop talking. He wanted to savor the image of the dark-haired girl smiling seductively at him. Perhaps he could slip a sleeping pill into Martha's after dinner drink tonight . . .

Stanley sipped iced tea. "Why not? You have a good life. You can see more of the world–"

"Look, Stanley, my wife and I have nothing in common. I have no intention of moving to some idiotic retirement village to wear slippers all day."

He shrugged. "If you feel that strongly, there's always divorce."

"Massachusetts is an 'equal division of property' state. Martha would get half of everything I've worked my ass off for."

"I see your point."

"From the time I was thirteen I worked. In college, I hustled for scholarships, waiting tables and driving a cab. My wife, on the other hand, led a privileged life of boarding schools and summer homes. Martha's never worked a day in her life. Her father gave her a generous allowance. When he died, most of his estate went to her."

"What happened to the money?" Stanley asked.

Arnold sighed. "Squandered on horses for the children, country club memberships, gardeners and swimming pools. The rest she invested in her brother's real estate development." He snickered. "A hurricane in the Keys washed everything away. The idiot didn't have flood insurance." He stared at his drink. "I'll be honest, Stan . . . sometimes the grave looks good. My wife will be around for a long time."

"I wouldn't be too sure of that," Stanley said quietly.

Arnold stared at him. "Are you trying to tell me something?"

Stanley returned his gaze. "I could be."

Arnold leaned across the table and grabbed the man's arm. "I'm drunk now, but I'm serious about this. I'll pay anything."

Stanley extricated his arm from Arnold's grasp. "We're not to speak of it. In one month I'll call your office and leave a message. I'll be Mr. Miller, a paper salesman. If you still feel the same way, you'll call the number back. The following month we will meet briefly at an arranged location. Until then you will not attempt to contact me. Failure to heed my instructions will sever all relations, understand?"

Arnold nodded, silent.

"End of conversation, then." He indicated Arnold's plate. "If you're not going to eat that sandwich, may I have it?"

"Be my guest." Arnold said, pushing the plate toward him.

He got up from the table and walked unsteadily to the bar. He wanted to tell the dark haired girl that yes, he'd meet her tonight, Martha be damned. But the young people were gone. In their place was a group of local fishermen drinking beer and watching TV.

Back at the table, Stanley said, "Tide's high. Let's get a move on."

From his seat in the bow, Arnold smiled as the sea breeze tousled his hair. The late afternoon colors washed over him. He felt as weightless and free as the sea gulls gliding above. For a while he swayed with the rhythm of the boat until the droning of the engine reverberated in his head. He closed his eyes and clutched the boat's sides, groaning aloud. Soon the boat slowed and finally came to a sputtering stop.

"Arnold, are you sick?"

He nodded, attempting to focus on Stanley in the rear of the boat. This made him dizzy.

"Let's move you back here. There's too much motion up front."

He opened his eyes to find Stanley hovering over him, his legs braced against the sides of the swaying boat. When Stanley lifted him to his feet, Arnold felt as floppy as the monkfish his stepfather had caught. Arnold remembered the creature's bulging, accusing eyes. He whimpered as Stanley gripped his upper arms. "Now I'm going to turn you," he said, his voice in Arnold's ear.

Arnold felt himself swiveling, but instead of being lowered to the rear of the boat, he was falling over the side, into the water. He came to the surface, choking and coughing. "Can't swim," he gasped.

"I know. Your wife told me."

"Help." Water ran into his nose and down his throat. He tried kicking his legs; they were as heavy as wooden pilings. Why wasn't Stanley helping him?

"Understand, it's nothing personal, Arnold. Martha contacted me six months ago. She's upset that you're not cooperating with plans for your golden years." He chuckled. "You know how women are. They view retirement as a second honeymoon."

"Help me."

Stanley must have moved; his voice, full of concern, came from further away. "I put something in your drink at the restaurant. You won't feel much."

"Help me," Arnold said, his voice drowned out by the boat's engine roaring to life.

"Don't worry, Arnie," Stanley called, "I won't tell Martha what you discussed. No sense in being unkind."

Arnold watched the boat as it slowly circled. This made him dizzy, so he closed his eyes. When he opened them, Stanley was gone. He squinted into the sun sinking into the water. Its surface glittered like a field of diamonds. For an instant he remembered the jewel in the navel of the girl with dark hair.

But only for an instant . . .

"BLUEFISH WEATHER"

"Janice! Where's my thermos?"

The voice blasted her out of a deep sleep. It was six a.m.. She sat up in bed, disoriented. Why was her husband calling her at this hour? Then she remembered: it was the first day of Roger's vacation. As always, he was going fishing.

She swung her legs out of bed, scuffing her feet across the sandy floor, feeling for her slippers. Though it was August, the non-insulated cottage was cool in the morning. During the winter it was arctic; the heat from the little wood stove never reached the bedroom on the second floor, and it was not unusual for her to go to bed wearing a knitted cap.

Janice didn't bother with her bathrobe. If she didn't reach the kitchen fast and help her husband find his thermos, he would start bellowing again and wake up her father. Her father was eighty-five years old. If he woke up, he'd insist on getting up. The sleeping pill he took every night wouldn't have worn off, and he'd not only be agitated, he'd be confused.

She walked into the kitchen to the welcome smell of coffee. The Mr. Coffee gurgled and hissed. Next to it, Roger's tackle box sat on the counter. He was flinging open cupboard doors and slamming drawers.

"Where's my goddamn thermos? I can't go fishing without my thermos!"

Janice ignored him. She knelt in front of the sink, pulled open a bottom drawer, and removed a large, scarred metal thermos. Holding onto the sink she got to her feet.

"I washed it for you. It smelled sour."

Roger grabbed the thermos and hurriedly filled it with coffee, his back to her. "Don't touch my stuff, Janice. How many times do I hafta tell you?"

"Shh!" She tiptoed to a door next to the refrigerator. In the sliver of light peeking in from the bottom of the window shade she could see her father in bed. His profile was sharp against the pillow. Even after she gently closed the door, she could hear his snoring.

"Chrissake," Roger said, fitting the thermos into his green tackle box, "those sleeping pills would knock out a buffalo. You trying to get rid of him permanently?"

Janice decided to ignore the remark. Roger was most likely hung over and trying to get her goat. He was not the one who got up in the middle of the night to calm her father when he woke up frightened and disoriented. If she didn't give her dad a sleeping pill, he'd attempt to get out of bed. Should he fall at his age, he'd break a hip or leg and that would be the end for him.

"Will you be home for dinner?" she asked. Roger was at the front door. Over his shoulder she saw the sun, a shimmering ball of fiery orange, coming up over Thatcher Island.

He paused to fish a cigarette out of a wrinkled pack. "Depends on how many bluefish I catch. It it's good, I'll be home early, maybe throw a couple on the grill. Otherwise I'll stay at the marina for a while, check out the boats."

She shivered in the salt breeze that blew in through the open door. "Good luck."

Janice crept back up the stairs. She had another hour or two before her father woke up. She burrowed back under her blankets. She knew Roger wouldn't be home for dinner. The Granite Cove Bluefish Tournament was on and she didn't expect to see much of him all week. If he wasn't sitting on the dock with his cooler, he'd be at the marina, flattering the women, shooting the breeze with his fellow fishermen, and drinking all night. Any

fish he caught he'd give away. They would never end up, brushed with butter and lemon, on her grill. Indeed, it had been a long time since she had
eaten fresh-caught bluefish.

For the millionth time in her six year marriage she wondered how she'd
ever gotten into such a mess.

"Janice! Janice!"

Roger stood on the beach waving his red tee shirt. She spotted him
through the front window when she came out of the kitchen carrying a
saucer of sliced bananas. Out on the back porch her father sat, a TV tray
before him.

"I'll be right back, Dad. I'm going down to the beach for a minute.
Roger's calling me."

"Who?"

"Roger," she said, leaning close to his ear. Her father always ended up
removing his hearing aid.

"Oh, him. Well, take your time, dear."

He'll tell me that, she thought, hanging her apron on a hook in the
pantry, and then two minutes later he forgets and starts calling to me.
Taking care of an old person was as much work as caring for a baby,
though she'd never had a baby, despite attempts to get pregnant. Actually, caring for an elderly person was more work; a baby became inde-
pendent and required less care, while an old person needed more and
more attention.

Two years ago Roger had talked about putting her dad in a nursing
home. "We can sell the cottage to a developer, Jan. We can travel anyplace."
Her head full of images of an open convertible whizzing along the Gulf,
she had broached the subject with her father. Even though he claimed he
didn't want to be a burden, he'd looked so sad–like a kid discovering his pet
dog had been run over. Janice knew she would never be able to make that
decision no matter how helpless he got. She couldn't ship her father off to
a home. He was all she had.

The sands were dotted with colorful beach umbrellas. Standing at the railing, she looked down at the crowds spread over the sand. Every summer more people discovered Granite Cove. Everyone wanted to rent one of the cottages that lined the boardwalk. Janice's father had bought the place forty years ago, in the 1950s, for $4,000. Today they could get at least $300,00 for the place, as shabby as it was. People were willing to pay that price for the pleasure of looking out at the moon shining on the water—right in their front yard.

Yet things at the beach had changed over the years. More cottages had cropped up on the boardwalk, along with condos and A-frames, totally out of place among the old fashioned shingle-style wooden structures. The wild rose bushes that grew rampant and the tall beach grass that she used to hide in were gone, replaced with crisp lawns like wall-to-wall carpeting.

At the creek end of the beach, shops had sprung up around the new condo buildings. They sold tee shirts, fried dough, bikinis and rubber rafts. The stately old wooden hotel where her parents had taken her for dinner had been torn down and replaced with a squat motel that hosted Sunday beer festivals. The police were often called to break up fights. Some nights she could hear the raucous music drifting out from the bar. While she didn't approve of the noisy establishment, Roger did. He liked to walk over to the bar at night. Of this Janice approved: at least he wasn't driving home drunk.

The Trupiano sisters, who rented the "Cozy Nook," a bungalow style cottage, were of an undetermined age. Janice guessed they were in their early forties. Although their bodies were hard from regular workouts, their skin was leathery from frequent sun-bathing. Even when swimming, the sisters wore jewelry: earrings, gold chain necklaces and ankle bracelets.

Now Lila and Lola Trupiano, wearing bikinis, sat in beach chairs, the intense rays of the noon sun reflecting off their dark, oiled skin. The pair held plastic glasses which Roger was in the process of filling from his metal thermos. He sucked in his stomach as he poured. At forty-five, he was still a handsome man, although the boozing was taking its toll. His strong jaw line was losing its clean definition and his cheeks, so ruddy from a distance, were a fine crosshatching of tiny broken veins.

To say Roger had been "neighborly" toward the Trupiano sisters would be an understatement. He was often at their cottage, repairing a malfunctioning refrigerator or fixing the VCR. "I can't help it if I'm a people person. I'm not like you, Janice, always judging everyone."

Sometimes, on her husband's invitation, the Trupiano sisters had cocktails on Janice's porch. They exclaimed loudly over everything–it was all adorable in their eyes: the old wicker rocker, the painted buoys, even her father himself.

Now, spotting Janice standing above them on the seawall they gestured frantically for her to come down. "You're missing the sun!" one of the sisters yelled. Visitors never understood how it was for the residents who lived at the beach year-round; they couldn't believe Janice preferred not to bake in the sun every day.

"Janice," Roger got up from his chair, "get me the corkscrew." The cooler was open, revealing mounds of glistening ice packed around frosty bottles.

One of the sisters: Lola/Lila turned in her chair. Her breasts almost parted company with the top of her bathing suit. "We're gonna make sangria," she shouted. "Come on down, okay? And bring your daddy."

Janice shook her head. "It's his nap time," she called. They thought it was so easy–just bring him down on the beach. And how was she supposed to get him down the narrow steps–by airlift?

Roger made a face at his wife. He held a dripping can of beer pressed against his furry chest. In a loud voice, he said, "Mother Theresa can't take a break. She's got diaper detail."

The sisters shrieked, covering their mouths, their shoulders shaking with laughter. As Janice turned and walked back to the cottage, she heard: "Oh, Roger, you are *wicked!*"

Russ, her neighbor, sat on his front porch watching his grandchildren jump off the porch railing into the sand. "Watch me, Grandpa!" they shrieked, lining up to take turns. He waved lazily to Janice as she walked up her steps. Janice wondered what the neighbors thought of her marriage. Many of the older residents had known her since she was a child. They had loved her mother and father. She remembered the clambakes and cook-outs the families organized, the babies crawling around in the sand.

Most likely the neighbors had assumed Janice would stay single. Although she was attractive, after thirty-five she'd given up on finding a mate. She knew the type of marriage she wanted, one like her parents had shared. It had been a courtly, old fashioned union. Her father always remembered to observe the niceties–to take his wife's arm on the street, to pull her chair out. When something puzzled him, he would remark to Janice, "Let's ask Mother, shall we?"

An only child, she'd had a close relationship with her parents. Their lives together, especially during winters at the beach when most of the cottages were boarded up, had been special. She remembered sitting around the wood stove in the kitchen, or standing at the ice encrusted railing and looking out at the gray winter ocean with snow-topped Thatcher Island in the distance.

Her family shared this winter world with other denizens of the beach, the sandpipers and seagulls, plus an occasional dog from town who would come to their door knowing her dad was good for a handout.

Janice had gone to a small agricultural college, majoring in greenhouse management. She loved growing things; at the beach, she kept pots of nasturtiums and flower boxes filled with portulaca. The neighbors claimed that if Janice couldn't coax something out of the sandy soil, no one could.

When her mother died, she was glad to have her job at the flower shop. The last year of her mother's life, when she'd stayed home and cared for her, had been a long and draining ordeal. After that experience she had no interest in going out on dates with immature men who acted like little boys.

Until one spring day, with the daffodils nodding in the sunshine, Roger had walked into her shop. He was all dressed up in a Madras sports jacket, but all she could see were his eyes, the color of the sea in May.

While he admired the flowers, she had on impulse handed him a purple iris for his lapel. She had even pinned it there, inhaling his lime cologne. Her boldness was uncharacteristic; Janice was shy around men, especially one as handsome as Roger. She thought to herself, Here was a man of experience. Indeed, there was nothing boyish about Roger. He had been around. For some reason, Janice was dazzled by the idea. She forgot why Roger had come into the shop: to buy a dozen roses for someone special, he'd said. Janice allowed herself to think the handsome stranger was buying roses for her.

Later, after they'd been married for a couple of years, she asked him who he had been dating when he walked into her flower shop. At first Roger didn't know what she was talking about. He'd been leaning over the pool table in the basement, about to place a shot and didn't answer at first. After sinking the ball in the pocket, he lit a cigarette and frowned in the act of remembering.

"Roses . . . roses," he mused, tapping the cue stick against his knuckles. "If it was roses, it must have been Pamela, the rich broad from Eastern Point." Turning his back to Janice and resuming his position, he said, "Yeah, if it was roses, it must have been her."

On his second visit to the flower shop, he was dressed in a tee shirt. He bought a single geranium and asked Janice if she wanted to go for a ride in his boat after work.

Watching Roger's convertible peel out of the parking lot, Janice felt she had stepped into a movie and her life had finally begun . . .

Regrettably, she hadn't remained in that state for long. Her new husband, she discovered, liked to buy cocktails for fair-haired women in dark bars. She reminded herself that life wasn't like a Disney movie. Happy endings were reserved for make-believe people like Snow White or Cinderella.

"There are no guarantees in life," her mother used to say. "All we have is hope."

Tattered hope at that.

She found her father in the kitchen, standing supported by his alumi-num walker. "Where were you, Janice? I called and called."

His knuckles, clutching the handles, were white, his forehead beaded with sweat. She eased him back to the cool porch, feeling guilty for leaving her father alone and unattended for so long. What if he had attempted to go down the back stairs?

She got him settled in the wicker rocker and smoothed a blanket over his lap. She held his hand until he fell asleep. In the distance, over the cry of the seagulls she heard, "Janice! Janice!" Then she remembered: Roger had asked for a corkscrew. She slowly removed her hand from her sleeping father's grip.

She heard the music from the radio long before she saw the trio on the beach. They were singing along: *"Roll out those lazy, hazy, crazy days of summer . . ."* Roger was standing, legs apart, twisting his hips to the music. He wore one of the sisters' straw hats with floppy flowers on the brim. The Trupiano sisters waved their arms over their heads, snapping their fingers to the beat.

When the sharp, spiraling end of the metal corkscrew landed inches away from Roger's foot, he immediately stopped singing. He stared down at the object as though it had fallen to earth from a UFO.

The sisters, sensing a change in mood, stopped singing *" . . . those days of soda and pretzels and beer . . ."*

"The hell, Janice."

Roger stuck his beer can into the sand and slowly walked to the seawall until he was standing directly below his wife. The sisters silently watched. He whipped off his mirrored sunglasses. The skin around his eyes was pale in contrast to his fiery red nose. He shaded his bloodshot eyes and looked up at her, a dark silhouette against the afternoon sun.

"What's the story, Jan?" he asked quietly.

"Dad's alone. I've got to get back to him. You want anything else?"

"I want an explanation of why you just tried to spear me. Are you gonna tell me or do I have to come up there and persuade you?"

"Look, Roger, it was an accident. You know I've got lousy aim." She glanced at the sisters smoking cigarettes, their faces expressionless.

Finally one yelled to Roger, "What about that sangria you promised?"

Roger turned around slowly as though remembering where he was. He bent and pulled the corkscrew out of the sand and shook it in the air like a sword. "Now you're talking!"

The sisters squealed with joy, happy that the good mood had been restored. This time they didn't ask Janice to join them.

The wheelchair kept sinking into the sand bordering the narrow concrete walkway. Janice managed to push her father past the last row of cottages until she reached the dusty parking lot. Wiping sweat from her forehead, she opened the passenger door of the car. Now for the tricky part–transferring her father from the chair into the front seat of her car. Following that, the awkwardness of folding the wheelchair and squeezing it into the trunk.

Despite the early evening hour, heat poured out of her car when she opened the door. At that moment Russ crossed the lot, wiping his hands on his shorts. He didn't ask if he could help, he just took over the operation, getting her dad to his feet, rotating his body, and finally lowering him into the front seat. Then he folded the wheelchair and put it in the trunk.

He tugged on the visor of her dad's Red Sox cap. "Going in town to the Bluefish Tournament, slugger?"

"I've won it many years," he said, squinting up at Russ.

"That's right," Janice said. "He was an ace sea captain."

"I had three boats," he said, coming out of his stupor to talk excitedly. "Gill netters. We used to go out for a whole week. I had some nice fellas working for me then. Real nice." His voice trailed off.

"Good for you," Russ said. He turned to Janice. "Is Roger in the blue-fish tourney?"

"He'll be the first one at the dock tomorrow morning," she said. "He's been fishing all week." She was certain Russ knew what else he'd been doing, but her neighbor merely smiled.

"You two have fun in town," he said.

Driving into town, Janice felt her spirits brighten. She'd been feeling glum lately. She couldn't afford to fall into a slump with so much work to do. I mustn't lose faith in myself, she thought. After all, her father wasn't going to live forever. She glanced at her dad, who looked pleased to be going out, and felt a stab of guilt.

Still, she had to prepare for the future. The money from the eventual sale of their cottage would buy a florist shop—with maybe room for a small apartment. Her dad wanted her to be happy. The only way she could get away from Roger was by selling the cottage. It would be like selling off her childhood, but she had to make a new life. Surely she could hold out until then. One day at a time, she reminded herself.

The Bluefish Festival attracted crowds every year. Tonight they clogged the streets. Wherever she looked there were tourists. Many were at the wharf snapping photos of the boats decorated with flags and lights. Sidewalk vendors sold cotton candy, pretzels and sausage rolls. Music blared from the open doorways of the bars lining the street. Teenagers threw firecrackers into the road.

As Janice inched along in the traffic, she saw her husband, his arms around the Trupiano sisters, crossing the street in front of the car before her. The sisters, in tight pants and tank tops, teetered in high heeled sandals. Roger wore the straw hat, its brim tilted over one eye.

She shrank back into the seat and to distract her father, she pointed and asked, "What's the name of that boat with the orange flags?"

"Looks like the Lady Grace," he said, squinting at the ship. A moment later he said, "No, that went down in '65."

"Do you mind if we don't stop downtown?" she asked. "I don't see a parking space and the sidewalks look too crowded for a wheelchair."

"I don't mind. Too many people anyway. Never used to be like this."

As they continued down the main thoroughfare, Janice kept her eyes straight ahead. Spotting a break in the traffic, she turned up the side street and headed back toward the beach. When they were finally on the shore road, her father, his eyes closed, said, "Don't worry about him, dear. Things will work out."

Janice glanced at him. Was it possible he'd seen Roger in the street? "Who's that, Dad?"

He said nothing more.

She rummaged through the kitchen cupboard, pushing aside jars of mustard, and bottles of ketchup and steak sauce. Her dad's sleeping pills were missing. For the second time Janice searched the shelves for the plastic vial. Could her father have pocketed them? He'd been up and around yesterday. She knew about depression in the elderly–was he planning something?

She looked at him sitting at the kitchen table, his thin fingers wrapped around a cup of warm milk. The overhead lamp cast deep shadows on his face. She knew he hated being dependent. He hated being unable to walk down the stairs unassisted or dress and feed himself properly. But did this make him want to end it all?

Janice would keep an eye on him and tomorrow, while he was on the back porch, go through his clothing and bedding until she found the pills.

That night she dreamed a huge fish approached her while she was swimming. Panicked, she was about to swim away when the fish opened its mouth. A bottle of pills lay inside.

Janice sat up in bed. She heard the waves crashing on the shore. She heard the frogs croaking at the salt marsh. Downstairs, a door closed. Wrapping a terry robe around her, she crept down the stairs, guided by the light of the moon shining into the living room.

Roger was in the kitchen. His back to her, he methodically spooned coffee into the pot. Coffee grounds littered the floor. His tackle box sat open on the kitchen counter, the thermos next to it.

Speaking softly, she said, "Turn off the light when you're through. And please try not to wake Dad."

He turned to stare at her through bleary eyes. His face was pale under the tan. "Don't creep up on me like that, Janice. And don't tell me what to do."

"I'm just asking you not to make any noise."

He grabbed the thermos and turned on the faucet. Water splashed over him as he tried to fill the opening. "Your father won't wake up, all the drugs you give him. He sleeps like a dead man."

"He could wake up now. I couldn't find his pills tonight." She narrowed her eyes. "You don't know anything about that, do you?"

Roger turned and winked. His face had the stunned expression of a drunk. "Wouldn't you like to know. Why not give him the whole bottle? What kind of life is that–can't take a leak without his daughter pulling down his pants. Bag of bones. Better off dead if you ask me."

"I didn't ask you," she said. "And if you don't approve, why don't you move in with your bimbos? Why stay here with us?"

Roger turned off the faucet. He carefully wiped his hands on a dishtowel. His voice was very quiet. "You'd like that, wouldn't you, Janice? You'd like me to leave so you can sell this place. I know what you have in mind." He pointed a finger at her. "Just you remember this: my name is on the deed, too. When we took out that loan to make repairs? The bank wouldn't give us the money unless my name was on the deed, too."

Janice remembered all the paperwork when they took out a loan after the storm. She didn't remember signing anything regarding the deed. There had been so many forms Roger had given her to sign. She'd been grateful he was handling it. It dawned on her–why else would he be so helpful?

Roger turned away, chuckling. "You broads are so dumb."

The next day was hot and muggy. Janice swept the front porch while at the same time swatted the greenheads that flew in from the marsh. On the beach, the Trupiano sisters, their vacation nearing an end, lay motionless, like beached manatees. All day the weather stayed torpid, the beach strangely quiet as a lassitude crept over its sands.

Her father sat on the back porch, oblivious to the buzzing greenheads that bounced off the screen. He slept, slack mouthed, and snored. Janice sat in the chair next to him, fanning herself with a magazine. Roger couldn't understand why they didn't have air conditioning.

"No one at the beach has air conditioning," she'd told him. "People come here for the salt breeze."

"The new condos at the creek have air conditioning," he'd said. Roger had been talking a lot about the new condos, a huge stucco building with a blue Mediterranean style plastic roof. He'd even gone for a tour with the Trupiano sisters. Janice had dismissed his interest at the time. Now it occurred to her . . . could he force a sale of her cottage?

Her father opened his eyes and blinked at Janice as if trying to place her. "Too hot out there," she said. "I don't suppose it'll be good fishing weather."

He closed his eyes. She thought he'd fallen asleep, but he said, "This is bluefish weather."

Janice sat listening to the flies hitting the screen. She must have dozed off because she awakened to the sound of the sheets on the clothesline snapping in a wind that had suddenly come up. People lugging beach gear hurried down the walkway trying to escape the big drops of rain that darkened the concrete.

She got up and went inside to look out the window. On the beach, a line of gray clouds gathered on the horizon. Seagulls stood in silent clusters at the water's edge. Heat lightening flashed in the distance. After she ushered her father into the darkening house, she ran from room to room closing the windows against the wind and rain. When the house was secured, father and daughter sat at the table, listening to the raging wind.

While she was heating his milk on the stove, she heard a loud knocking at the door. Her dad reached for his walker. "I'll see who that is."

"You sit right there," she said. "It's probably Russ wanting to use our phone."

She approached the door and saw, through the window above, a figure in oilskins standing outside. Behind him, lightening flashed on the water. The wind that blew in with him smelled strongly of seaweed.

"Ma'am, I'm Cal Devine. Police department. Can I come in?"

Janice recognized the cop from his weekend patrols on the beach where he was kept busy kicking noisy teenagers and their kegs from the beach. At the same time, he was also quick to help mothers carry their baby strollers down the stairs. "Come in. Come in." She shut the door against the wind. "Let me take your jacket."

Officer Devine's yellow poncho dripped on the floor when he took it off. "Sorry about the mess," he said, and nodded to Janice's father at the table. "Evening, sir," he said loudly.

"Sit down, officer," Janice said, motioning to the table.

"Thanks. Maybe you should sit, too." His voice was quiet.

Instead, she stood behind her father's chair. "I'm all right. You have bad news, don't you? Is it about my husband?"

"I'm afraid it is. I know Roger . . . knew your husband from the marina. I keep a little boat there myself." He pulled a notebook from his pocket and opened it. "He was the owner of the Lady Godiva?"

She could see the cop didn't want to tell her. She gripped the back of her father's chair. "Yes. What happened to my husband?"

He took a handkerchief from his pocket and wiped the back of his neck where rain dripped down his collar. He looked from Janice to her father. "The Coast Guard found him earlier. Storm washed his boat aground on Thatcher Island. The medical examiner thinks he'd had a heart attack or a stroke."

"Are you sure?" She reached for the chair next to her and sat. Roger? How could it be?

The cop glanced at his notebook. "They tested his blood for alcohol. We won't know the results yet, but it might be a factor. We found an empty bottle in his boat." He gave her a thin smile. "It's festival week. Everyone in town gets a little crazy this time of year." He closed his notebook and put it back in his pocket. "I made a positive ID, but you'll have to verify that. Would you like me to take you?"

"Do I have to go now?"

"In the next few hours. Do you want an autopsy? The coroner will do it at your request."

Janice closed her eyes. "No, I don't think so."

"God, no," her dad said, putting his hand over hers.

"I'm sorry to ask, but did your husband take drugs?"

"Drugs? Of course not. Roger was a . . . drinker."

The cop shook his head. "Bad combination, alcohol and the sun. Yet people do it all the time–get dehydrated and don't even know it." He stood up. "If you wait a minute, I'll get his tackle box from the cruiser."

When the door closed behind him, Janice turned to her father. "Dad, I can't believe this is happening."

He patted her hand. "A nice cop," he said, watching the door.

When Officer Devine returned carrying the green tackle box, Janice averted her eyes. "Where do you want this?" he asked.

Janice pointed to the kitchen. "In there. On the floor."

Moments later the cop picked up his poncho from the chair. He cleared his throat. "I'm sorry, ma'am. Don't forget to come in to make an ID. Since you're not requesting an autopsy, what we do is call Limone's Funeral Home, unless you have someplace else in mind."

Janice shook her head. She thanked the man and saw him to the door. As she watched him descend the front steps, her dad called out: "Is my hot milk ready?"

She sighed. Not even a death in the family could keep him from his routine. "Just a minute."

She entered the kitchen. Officer Devine had shoved the tackle box between the sink and refrigerator. Janice turned on a back burner to reheat the saucepan of milk. After pouring it into a mug, she hastily set it before her father, spilling some on the table and not bothering to wipe it.

"Dad, I've got to walk and clear my head. You sit here and don't move. I'm only going to the end of the boardwalk." He nodded. She knew he wanted to ask for his bedtime cookie, but something in his daughter's voice silenced him.

She threw on her yellow slicker, pulling the hood over her hair. Outside, the rain had let up but not the wind. She walked fast, one hand clinging to the metal railing, pulling herself along. The roaring surf drove all thoughts from her mind as she walked numbly along the shoreline.

When she reached the end of the boardwalk, she stood and watched the rushing water overflowing the creek bed. She felt the first spasm of remorse. She'd wanted to end her marriage, but not like this. She'd never imagined anything like this. Although their union hadn't been close, she suspected that Roger, for all his bluster, had feared true intimacy. She wiped the tears that filled her eyes.

When she finally returned to the cottage she saw, through the front window, her father's empty chair at the table. His walker, too, was gone. She ran up the steps.

"Dad?" she called at the door.

She heard water running in the kitchen and rushed across the room. In the dim light from the dining room, she saw her father at the kitchen sink, his forearms supported by the walker. Steam rose around him, dampening his thin white hair. He hadn't heard her calling. He was scrubbing, showing an energy Janice hadn't seen in years. He was washing her late husband's metal thermos, scouring it vigorously, as though his life depended on it . . .

"MEN OF MEANS"

Often they bring me a single red rose. It is so touching–as if I'm their sweetheart and not someone who advertises for men. Here's how it works: I place an ad in the personals section: *Wanda, young, blonde and bashful, wishes to meet men of means. Big surprise waiting.*

When they call, I arrange a meeting site–somewhere secluded where we can get acquainted in private. They approve of my discretion; after all, they're married.

On the day of our rendezvous, I arrive early and hide among the trees. From this vantage point I study them carefully: Is that a Burberry coat he's wearing? Custom-made shoes? A Rolex? Nice tie. I'll bet she picked it out.

At the right moment I appear in my miniskirt and high-heeled boots. How their eyes light up! Before long we retire to the privacy of their car. Eventually I hear the stories: the money-grasping wives, the ungrateful children . . .

Of course they never ask about *me*. What do they care? Should they inquire, they'd discover that I have a black belt and a criminal record, and that I hate red roses and cheaters. And once they learn what's beneath my skirt, they pay attention.

Oh yes, they do . . .

"A NICE ITALIAN GIRL"

From the back seat of the taxi, Sofia watched the workman making final adjustments to the sign over the front door of the restaurant. Finally he flipped a switch, illuminating the neon sign. In hot pink letters, it read: *Nina's Trattoria*.

Sofia nodded. The sign looked good. It symbolized the restaurant's transformation from Old World traditional to contemporary cool. Nina's place would attract the young money crowd, professionals who wouldn't balk at paying $25 for a plate of gnocchi.

Not only had the restaurant changed, Nina herself had undergone a transformation from immigrant kitchen worker to savvy businesswoman. Aunt Sofia had taught her well . . .

As the cab driver dozed in the front seat, Sofia wrapped her shawl around her and watched the customers arriving. The men wore fitted suits and the women high heels and gold jewelry. Sofia admired their easy confidence. They wouldn't be awed by the restaurant's sophisticated interior, its upscale cuisine.

It wasn't always the case. Not long ago, when Sofia inherited the place from her mother, it had been called, simply, Mama's. Back then it didn't have the leather chairs and oil paintings on the walls.

It didn't have the wine cellar either . . .

When she was a little girl, Sofia would run home after school to find her mother in the kitchen of the family's North End restaurant. Mama would put a bowl of minestrone soup on the table. Sofia would eat while doing her homework. Occasionally early diners would arrive: tourists drawn by the savory smells of Mama's Eggplant Rotini wafting from the door: More often it was the regulars, the old men who sat at the tiny bar and drank strong coffee and Chianti. Seeing Sofia's dark head bent over her books, they would ask what she wanted to be when she grew up.

She never hesitated: "I want a restaurant just like Mama's, only bigger."

Her mother would shake her head while her father would say, "My Sofia is not only beautiful, she's a hard worker. Just you wait."

In high school, Sofia worked in the kitchen along with a collection of cousins newly arrived from Italy. Later her niece Nina joined them. While the cousins struggled with the language, Nina picked it up quickly. She understood when Mama barked: "Grate more Parmigiano!" or "Watch the sauce!"

The kitchen was tiny and hot, making Sofia's dark curls frizz around her face. On a Saturday night there was no room to move about. Cases of wine were stacked everywhere. After repeatedly banging her shins, Sofia approached her father, "Papa, we need a wine cellar."

He chuckled. "My Sofia has big ideas," he told the patrons.

After the last customers had drifted out and all that remained were the men, Sofia and Mama cleared a table in the back. They shared a bowl of pasta. Mama poured wine from a straw-covered bottle. Their conversation centered on the restaurant. "Everything cost so much in this city," Mama complained. "Maybe we should move."

Sofia was quick to dissuade her. "Someday we'll expand and have more customers. Then we'll build a wine cellar."

Mama shook her head. "Your father's heart is not strong enough."

"I'll do Papa's job. I'm strong enough for both of us."

Her mother patted her hand. "What a worker my little girl is."

Time passed, and Sofia's father complained of shortness of breath. He stayed home more, leaving Sofia to take over his job, greeting the customers and tending the little bar. Nina waited on the front tables while the young cousins cleared and worked in the kitchen.

"We need more space, Mama," Sofia said. The restaurant had gotten a good review in *Boston Magazine*, resulting in a line of people out the door on Friday nights. This time Mama didn't answer. She was too distracted. Sofia knew she was worried about Papa, whose color was poor. Later, Sofia talked it over with Nina. They decided that Mama would stay home and look after Papa. Sofia and Nina, along with the cousins, would handle the restaurant.

In return, Mama agreed to make Sofia a partner. "You're doing the work of three people. You're entitled to half."

The sign on the door of Mama's restaurant read: CLOSED FOR FUNERAL. Papa's heart had finally failed. Mama went into mourning, rarely appearing at her restaurant. When she did, something would reminded her of Papa and she'd collapse in tears. Now Sofia assumed her mother's role and began making decisions on her own, often discussing them with Nina, who'd become her assistant.

A year passed. The restaurant prospered under Sofia's management. She and Nina worked well together, each knowing what the other needed without having to ask. Mama continued to stay home. Sofia dropped by to see her when she could slip away. She had given up trying to get Mama to visit the restaurant. "Too many memories," Mama said. She spent her days watching soap operas and venturing out only to attend Sunday Mass. Father Gladiola, her priest, always had a sympathetic ear.

One Spring afternoon, with a fresh breeze blowing in from the harbor, Mama walked into the restaurant on the arm of a man. Sofia, polishing the espresso machine, stared in wonder. Nina, sitting at a table and copying the day's specials, blinked. Mama, no longer dressed in black, introduced Carlo Montillado, claiming that she'd met him at church.

Carlo wore a sharkskin suit and shiny black shoes. His body was soft, like the sacks of flour piled in the pantry. His nose was as sharp as a lobster claw and his skin was pitted like an orange. Nonetheless, he had a swagger, evident in the way he gazed around the restaurant, sizing it up.

"We're just stopping in for a minute," Mama said. "We won't get in your way."

"Can I get you anything?" Sofia asked, recovering from her surprise.

"Two Sambucca with coffee," Carlo said, steering Mama to a table in the back.

When Sofia set their drinks before them, Mama smiled at Carlo. "I told you my Sofia was beautiful, didn't I?"

"She takes after her mother," he said.

As she walked away, Sofia felt the man's eyes upon her. She escaped to the kitchen where the cousins were standing behind the door, gaping at Mama's high-heeled sandals and red toenail polish.

"That's enough," Sofia scolded. "Now get back to work."

Seconds later, Nina joined her in the kitchen. Without looking at Sofia, she said, "It's good to see Mama out and about, isn't it?"

But Sofia didn't respond. Standing at the kitchen door, she stared at the stranger holding her mother's hand.

Sofia finally decided not to interfere with Mama's friendship, to let her come to her senses. Her mother, a widow, was obviously flattered by a man's attention. Furthermore, her mother had a good head on her shoulders. Sofia knew she would eventually see through Carlo.

Yet ignoring the situation wasn't easy. All summer long Sofia heard rumors about Mama and Carlo—they were seen at the race track, or dancing at Wonderland Ballroom. One day, shopping at Haymarket, Sofia spotted them driving by in Carlo's convertible, his big arm circling Mama.

One night, shortly before closing, the couple made an appearance at the restaurant. Mama, laughing too loudly, showed off her new clothes to the cousins. Sofia retreated to the kitchen. *What would Papa say*, Sofia thought, peering out the door. She decided it was time to have a talk with her mother.

The following afternoon, Sofia visited her mother's apartment.

"When are you coming back?" she asked. "Everyone misses you. No one can make Eggplant Rotini like Mama, they say."

"Funny you should mention that," Mama said. "Carlo is a good cook. I've had dinner at his house. Perhaps we have a job for him."

Sofia stared. "Do you mean at our restaurant?"

"Of course, where else?"

"But . . . you hardly know him."

She laughed. "Look at your face, so stricken. I wouldn't ask Carlo if I didn't think he could help." Before Sofia could respond she said, "He used to be a maitre d' in Atlantic City. Carlo knows the restaurant business well."

Sofia felt her cheeks flush. Before she could stop herself, she blurted out, "I don't trust him."

Mama glared. "If you can't accept my friends, then perhaps we have nothing more to say."

Sofia didn't see her mother for weeks. One late night she told Nina about the conversation with Mama. "It's obvious to everyone he's up to something," Sofia said. "Not only that, the man's ten years younger. I can't believe my mother would be so . . . foolish."

"Don't be quick to judge. Perhaps Carlo will work out," she said.

Sofia stared at her niece. "You've always been honest with me, Nina. Do you really believe that?"

Nina sighed and patted Sofia's hand.

In order to avoid thinking about her mother, Sofia threw herself into running the restaurant. "Maybe this winter we'll close for a couple of weeks," she told Nina. "We'll finally get our wine cellar built."

She was feeling optimistic. There was less buzz about Mama and Carlo. Sofia hoped it meant her mother had finally come to her senses. But just when she began to relax, her world collapsed. One afternoon, one of the cousins arrived at work breathless to tell the news. While shopping on

Washington Street, she had spotted Mama, who claimed she was buying a wedding outfit.

The week after Labor Day, Sofia attended Mama's wedding. It was a small crowd of family and friends at the church. Sofia, a black lace mantilla covering her face, sat with Nina and watched as Father Gladiola performed the ceremony. Earlier, Sofia had visited the priest to privately express her concerns about Carlo.

He'd listened quietly and then said, "Your mother made a decision to share her life." With that, he touched Sofia's hand, forcing her to look at him. "God doesn't intend for us to mourn forever. He wants his children to be joyous." Later, Sofia learned that Carlo had donated a wide screen TV to the church rectory.

When the couple descended the church steps, they discovered Carlo's convertible had been decorated with streamers and a sign reading: JUST MARRIED. Everyone gathered on the sidewalk to see them off. Sofia stepped forward to give her mother a hug, asking where she was going on her wedding trip.

"We rented a cozy cabin on Lake Winnipesaukee," Mama said, smiling shyly.

"Did you bring a bikini to swim?" one of the cousins asked, causing the young girls to giggle.

Mama pretended to shiver. "I only swim in a hot tub."

Carlo helped Mama into the car before getting behind the wheel. The cousins threw rice and flower petals at the newlyweds. Before driving off, Carlo caught Sofia's eye. He winked.

The car roared away trailing streamers and balloons.

A week after the wedding, Sofia was in the kitchen stirring the sauce when she looked up to see Nina, white-faced, in the doorway.

"What is it, Nina?" Sofia untied her apron, letting it drop as she slowly approached her niece. "It's Mama, isn't it?" Nina continued to stare until Sofia took the younger woman by the shoulders and shook her. "Answer me!"

"The police were at the house," she said. "It's Mama . . . they said she drowned swimming in the lake."

Sofia pressed her hands to her head as though trying to force out Nina's words. "I knew it," she said. "I knew this would happen."

The only dry eyes at Mama's funeral were Sofia's and Father Gladiola's, the latter conducting the Mass. From behind her lace mantilla, Sofia observed the mourners. She breathed in the air heavy with candle wax and lilies. Her eyes traveled to the gleaming coffin. She refused to believe Mama was inside. No, her mother was back in the kitchen where she would always be. As if in a dream she heard Mama say, "Leave it to Sofia. She'll take care of everything."

Carlo sat slumped in the pew ahead of her. From time to time he sighed heavily, wiping his face with a lavender handkerchief that matched the iris worn in his lapel. Sofia looked beyond his big body to the casket covered with white lilies and pale yellow roses, the same flowers that had made up her mother's bridal bouquet.

Later, walking out of the church behind the coffin, Sofia clutched Nina's arm. They walked slowly past the mourners. Some tried to catch her eye. Others reached out, whispering her name. When she stumbled, Nina put a steadying arm around her.

"Be brave. Mama's watching," she whispered.

Sofia nodded. Of course Mama was watching.

Two weeks later, the restaurant opened under a new name: *Sofia's*. Customers arrived early. Everyone worked overtime in an effort to handle the hungry crowd. The crew carried steaming bowls of mussels and platters of antipasto back and forth through the kitchen's swinging door. "We need more space," Nina agreed.

One rainy Wednesday night after everyone had gone home Sofia was taking an inventory of the pantry. As she knelt before a tower of cans, the front door opened. "We're closed," she called out.

"Not yet," the voice responded.

Recognizing the raspy voice, Sofia slowly got to her feet. Carlo, wearing a white suit and Panama hat, stood in the doorway.

"I don't want you coming in here."

He walked unsteadily to the bar where he straddled a stool. "I want a Sambucca. No ice."

"If you don't leave, I'll call the cops."

"And what will you tell them?"

"I'll tell them you're trespassing."

He removed his hat and carefully placed it on the bar. Then he lit a cigarette. "How can I be trespassing when I own half this restaurant?"

Sofia stared at him. "What are you talking about?"

"I've seen a lawyer. As you know, your mother didn't leave a will. As her surviving spouse, I'm entitled to her estate." He blew a stream of smoke into the air. "Her estate is one half of this restaurant." He smiled. "I've stayed away out of respect for your feelings." His eyes traveled over her body. "It looks like you've lost some weight. I see it in your hips."

Sofia spun around and yanked a knife out of a wooden block. "Leave now or I'll kill you."

The big man leaned over the bar to grab the Sambucca bottle and a glass. He poured a generous amount. "You won't kill anyone, Sofia. You'd end up in jail and who'd run the restaurant then? No, you won't kill me. You're a nice Italian girl, just like your mama."

She returned the knife to the block. "What do you want?"

"What do I want? I want what's legally mine."

"You won't get a cent."

Carlo threw back the rest of his drink. He climbed off the bar stool, dropping his cigarette on the floor and grinding it with the toe of his shoe. Adjusting the brim of his hat, he said, "Sofia, I'm disappointed in you. Unless you agree to a buy out, it looks like I'm taking you to court."

"Don't push me, Carlo."

"Tell you what, I'll give you two weeks to think it over. Either buy me out or I'll force a sale on this place."

"You can't do that."

"Yes I can. It will all be explained in a letter from my lawyer." He headed for the door. "Think about it and let me know. I'll be in tomorrow night and the next. As a matter of fact, you can count on seeing a lot of Carlo." He cocked the brim of his hat. When he reached the door, he turned to look at her. "Sofia?"

She stared at him, silent.

"You'd better be nice to me." He winked. "After all, I'm your stepfather."

Long after he drove away, Sofia remained at the window, staring out at the dark, rainy street.

The following night she was beginning to think Carlo had been a bad dream until he sauntered in, taking a seat at the end of the bar.

"The last race just finished at Suffolk Downs," he said. "Sorry I'm late. Give me a bottle of your best Chianti." He lit a cigar despite the dirty looks from neighboring diners.

"I can give you a glass, but not a bottle," she told him. "We're closing soon."

"Go ahead and close. I'm not a customer, remember? " When she turned away, he called, "Where are the pretty cousins? I want to see them."

Sofia went into the kitchen. "He's here," she told Nina. "Let's try to get through this"

"Don't let him get to you," Nina said.

Carlo returned the next night, and the following. Whenever Sofia looked up, there he was, watching her. "Why don't you wear something sexy?" he asked, his voice low. "Don't you like to please men?"

Sofia ignored him. She knew how to handle drunks.

After a week of Carlo's visits, Nina sidled up to her in the kitchen while Sofia was counting receipts. "We have to talk," Nina said.

"I'm on my way to the bank."

"It's about the cousins."

"What about them?"

Nina sighed. "Carlo's been giving them fifty dollar tips. He's invited them to his apartment, claiming he's got a shipment of perfume and shoes."

"Are they going?"

"What do you think? They make so little working here. They're nice girls, but they're young."

Not for the first time Sofia wished Papa was still alive and tending bar. Papa would have thrown Carlo out the door, along with his hat.

The following night Sofia leaned across the bar. "We need to talk," she told Carlo.

"Talk about what?" His breath was heavy with garlic as he gazed down the front of her dress. "By the way, I'm glad you're taking my advice. You look like a woman tonight."

"I think we can hammer out an agreement over dinner, after we close. Are you free?"

He smiled. "Coming to your senses, are you? Your mother used to say you were a smart girl."

In the kitchen Sofia removed the platter of lobster ravioli from the refrigerator.

Nina raised her eyebrows. "We're closing. Who's that for?"

"For Carlo." She slid the plate into the warming oven. "For dinner, later."

Nina wiped her hands on her apron. "I'll stick around then. You'll need me."

"No, we're talking business. It's better we're alone."

Their eyes met. Nina patted her shoulder and said nothing.

That night, after the kitchen help had gone, Sofia was making last minute preparations when she spotted Carlo in the doorway.

"You look beautiful, Sofia," he said, taking in her short skirt and white peasant blouse. "Why hide a body like that?"

She motioned him to a table lit with candles in the back of the room. As he tucked a napkin under his chin, she emerged from the kitchen with antipasto, bread, and a bottle of Chianti.

"Sofia, sit and eat with me," he said, making a grab for her wrist.

"I must check on the ravioli." She poured him another glass of wine. "I'll join you in a moment." Although he was disappointed, Carlo's appetite took precedence.

Finally, after polishing off the last of the ravioli and wine, he sat back and loosened his belt. "Is there anything nicer than a beautiful woman who cooks like an angel?"

Sofia sat across from him and sipped her wine. "Shall we discuss business now?"

"Come sit over here near me."

"In a moment. First hear my proposition."

He twirled a toothpick in his mouth. "A proposition, eh?"

"A business proposition."

He waved her away. "It's always business with you Sofia. Why don't you act like a woman?"

Instead of answering, she removed a sheet of paper from her pocket and smoothed it out on the table. "I've got the figures here," she said. "I'm prepared to pay you $5,000 a month for two years. At the end you will have $120,000."

He frowned at the paper. "So?"

"One hundred twenty thousand is half of what the restaurant is worth."

Carlo reached for the Chianti. "You are like your mother—no head for business. In the first place, this restaurant could be worth a lot more if it's run properly. The way things are now, you'll never make money. Expand the bar, have music and dancing . . . booze. That's where the money is—not on ravioli." He reached across the table. "Let's be partners, Sofia. I don't want to cut you out."

"Cut me out?"

"If you don't go along with my plans, I'll have no choice but to force a sale. I own half. The lawyer said I can do it."

She was silent for a long moment. "So, you won't accept my offer?"

Carlo laughed. "For $60,000 a year? Sweetheart, I owe more than that to the loan sharks."

Sofia stood up, stuffing the paper into her pocket. "I've got to get the dessert. It's something special."

"Bring more Sambucca," he said.

Sofia took the thick slice of tiramisu from the refrigerator and put it on a plate. When she returned, Carlo looked up: "I'm glad to see you smiling. You look beautiful when you smile." When she placed the dish in front of him, he grabbed her wrist. "Sit here next to me. You're always rushing off." She moved to his side of the table and watched him scoop the cake into his mouth.

"Aren't you having any?" he asked.

"I'm watching my weight." She took a sip of her wine.

"The way you look, you drive men wild."

"Finish your tiramisu, Carlo. It's my specialty."

"I know what you're trying to do–butter me up. Put on some music, will you?"

Sofia got up and located the boom box in the kitchen. Soon the voice of Tony Bennett filled the room. Carlo lurched to his feet and grabbed her wrist.

"Let's dance."

She allowed herself to be led onto the floor where Carlo wrapped his arms around her and murmured in her ear, "You feel good, Sofia. Why have we been apart all this time?"

"You were married to Mama, remember?"

"Your mother was a nice lady, but it was you all along."

"Me? Didn't you love her?"

"Hey, don't get me wrong. Like I said, she was a nice lady. Anyway, when I set eyes on you, all bets were off."

She looked up at him. "You know, Carlo, I think Mama was foolish to go in that lake. Didn't she tell you she couldn't swim?"

"What can I say? You know how it is with broads and honeymoons."

"I understand you tried to save her."

"I almost died trying." He pressed her close, his big body enveloping hers.

"Still, it troubles me. Mama hated cold water and couldn't swim. She'd never been in lake water in her life."

He pulled away to look at her. "All this talk, Sofia. Let's enjoy the music." As Carlo extended his arm to twirl her around, he staggered.

"What's wrong?"

"Too much Sambucca. Let's sit down a minute." He reached for his chair and sank into it. "Get me some coffee," he said, shaking his head. "I feel woozy."

"I'll be right back," Sofia said, rising.

She grabbed the dishes and silverware and brought them to the kitchen. There she stuffed the remains of the tiramisu into the garbage disposal and scoured the plates in hot, soapy water. When the kitchen was presentable, she opened the pantry. Standing behind the door, she removed her skirt and blouse. She took a tee shirt and jeans from a hook inside the door and put them on.

When she checked on Carlo, he was slumped in his chair, his head resting on the table. Sofia listened to his snoring. Satisfied, she crossed the room to lock the front door and turn out the lights. Back in the kitchen, she grabbed a flashlight and headed for the cellar.

The light from her flashlight illuminated cobwebs hanging from the ceiling. In a far corner of the dirt cellar, a shovel stood next to a large hole in the ground. When she'd first started digging, it had seemed too great a task, but night after night she'd made progress. Now Sofia put on the familiar work gloves and picked up the shovel. If she kept at it, she would be finished before the morning sun reached the kitchen window.

Three hours later she removed her gloves to rub her calloused hands. She straightened her aching back. Holding the flashlight, she climbed the stairs. Upstairs, the candle had burned out. In the dim light from the outside street lamp, Carlo lay sprawled across the table, one arm hanging over the side. She forced herself to get close in order to listen to his breathing. He was deathly still.

She had worried that the pills she'd mixed into the tiramisu would be ineffective. She'd found them while cleaning out her mother's medicine cabinet. Fortunately, they hadn't lost their potency.

Now she turned to the unconscious man. Getting his body down the stairs would be a feat of strength.

She put on her gloves . . .

The following week Sofia kept the key to the cellar in her apron pocket. If someone needed an item from downstairs, she got it. The cousins merely shrugged their shoulders. Their boss was somewhat eccentric. Nina, on the other hand, asked no questions.

When Sofia later mentioned the proposed wine cellar, one of the cousins claimed to know a mason, a young man visiting from Sicily. Sofia hired him to pour the cement foundation. On the night he showed up to work, she took him into the cellar. Halfway down the stairs the smell reached him. He turned to Sofia with a questioning look.

"It's the sausage." She pointed to the rows suspended from the ceiling. At the same time, she slipped him $50.

They continued down the stairs.

At some point a Boston Police detective appeared at the restaurant, asking questions about Carlo. "I understand he's your stepfather?"

"He was briefly married to my mother," Sofia told him.

The detective wanted to know when they had seen him last.

"Here, at the restaurant," Nina said. She encouraged the man to sit and placed a glass of Chianti before him. "I'm afraid he was drunk," she added.

"He liked to gamble at the race track," Sofia said.

"He was deeply in debt," Nina said, sitting opposite the man and pouring more Chianti.

The detective scribbled in a notepad. "How do you know that?"

"He came here one night and pressured me to buy out his share in the restaurant," Sofia said. "He needed money badly."

"Do you think Carlo was involved with the Mafia?" Nina asked, leaning forward. "By the way, Detective, would you like to try some Shrimp Romana, my specialty?"

" I don't see why not." The man set aside his notepad.

When the wine cellar was finished, Sofia threw a small party for the regular customers. Taking her guests into the cellar, she proudly showed them around. Before turning out the light, she pointed to the engraved plaque on the wall. *In Memory of Mama,* it read.

Now Sofia tapped the cab driver's shoulder. "Logan International Airport," she said, settling back in the seat.

The driver started the car and pulled out into traffic. Sofia turned for a final look at the familiar skyline. She would miss Boston, though not the weather. The little house she had purchased in Italy had a lemon tree in the front yard. She looked forward to her new life.

As the cab made its way through the narrow cobblestone streets, she watched with mixed emotions. At that moment, a flock of birds emerged from a cherry tree. For an instant they hung suspended in the sky. Then they swooped, circled, and vanished into the clouds.

"THE GHOST OF WINTHROP HALL"

The story has all the elements of a classic mystery: an oceanside mansion, a beautiful young wife, her sailor husband, a shipwreck. What remains is the ghost and its lonely vigil. But first, a little background information:

In 1994, I was hired to be the editor in chief of the campus newspaper at Endicott College in Beverly, 20 miles north of Boston.

With Halloween approaching, I needed some "scary" stories and didn't have to look very far, for it seemed everyone had either heard—or witnessed—the Ghost of Winthrop Hall.

Among the many charms of Endicott's seaside campus are its buildings, many of them historically significant. Winthrop Hall, a sprawling edifice perched high above the Atlantic, served as a dorm. A Georgian mansion, it was named for John Winthrop, the first Governor of Massachusetts, and is one of the oldest houses on Boston's North Shore. A dungeon lies under the library floor, its door concealed. Years ago, slaves escaping to Canada were hidden there.

When I made inquiries about the ghost, I was told to speak to Denise Bilodeau, then Director of Student Development. She had reportedly seen "the lady in blue," as the ghost was called. Nonetheless, when I contacted her, she was reluctant to talk about ghosts, and certainly not for a newspaper. In any event, before hanging up she remarked, "By the way, it's the lady in pink, not blue."

With a deadline approaching, I reluctantly put the story aside, although I never lost interest in the intriguing ghost tale.

Five years later, while writing for a local newspaper, I decided to resume my investigation into the Winthrop Hall ghost and went straight to one of the earliest recorded sources: Eleanor Tupper, Ph.D., founder of Endicott College. In 1939, she wrote about the history of the school in her book, *Endicott and I* (Cricket Press, 1985).

Dr. Tupper, a no-nonsense professional with a strong Lutheran background, lived at Winthrop Hall with her family during her years as president of the college. On page 63 in her book she deals with the ghost in her characteristic head-on manner. She writes:

The students believed a legend that a beautiful lady dressed in blue came and went from the cellar area of Winthrop. Each year some girls would see her. One incident occurred that gave our family pause. Our daughter, Pricilla, then seven years old, had never heard talk of ghosts but one twilight she sat alone on the Winthrop porch near the stairs leading to the lawn. As she tells it, a "lady in blue" rounded the corner from the north side of the house and moved along the porch and approached her. The image was clear, not transparent, and Pricilla was looking calmly at first but then realized the lady had no legs and was unusually quiet. As the lady floated closer, Pricilla beat a hasty retreat. Since then, several students and a housemother have seen the unearthly visitor .

Perhaps the frightened young girl had mistaken the dress color. Those familiar with the ghost invariably say she is dressed in pink. On the other hand, maybe it is not unusual for ghosts to have a wardrobe change.

Liz Atilano, then director of the college's Career Center, enthusiastically discussed the "pink lady," as she called her. From 1981-83 Atilano was Resident Director of Winthrop Hall and familiar with the old mansion and its legends. According to Atilano, the ghost suffered from a broken heart:

"Many years ago, the young mistress of the house would pace the wide verandah that faces the open sea, hoping to catch a glimpse of her husband, whose ship sailed past on its way to Salem Harbor. Legend claims that a storm arose and she witnessed his boat become impaled upon the jagged rocks not too far from her porch. Alone and heartbroken, she hanged herself from the beams, leaving behind her ghost who continues to pace the corridors of the mansion."

Atilano claims that one of the ghost's trademark rituals involves a painting hanging in the foyer. It is a landscape of a tree and its reflection in a pond. When the ghost is present, the painting can be found turned upside down. "I have seen the painting turned many times, and each time I heard her footsteps. When I was alone in the building, I'd hear keys rattling. Students told me of seeing her," she said.

Yet Atilano never considered the ghost to be a threat. "It wasn't like the movies. She was never scary. There were no moans and groans. I felt she was there to welcome us."

Pink ladies or pink elephants? A cynic would assume the latter, although the people I interviewed were level-headed individuals. In fact, a former police officer confirmed the story. Al Cipriani, a retired Beverly police officer who'd joined the college's maintenance department, had heard the eerie tales. And while he never directly saw the ghost, he was aware of its presence. It was while working at Winthrop Hall during the summer when the college was closed.

"My buddy and I were alone in the house, working downstairs in the rec room. We kept hearing footsteps above us and on the stairs. The house was locked. There was no one but us in the building. Tell you the truth, it was kind of spooky."

It is not surprising that ghost stories should arise from the area in question. After all, the land dates back to the Puritans and plays an important role in the Witch Trials of neighboring Salem. Archives at Endicott's library contain background information on the land surrounding the college.

It was a crisp autumn day when I sat down with a bulging folder containing old, faded records collected by local and college historians. What I learned helped explain the ghost story in terms of the area from which it evolved. Attention is focused on the woods behind Endicott College.

On maps both old and current, the area is called Witches' Woods, named for those accused of witchcraft years ago in nearby Salem. These tortured individuals sought shelter in the great expanse of dark, dense woods. One historian writes: "The woods were thought to be haunted."

Around that time, the daughter of wealthy landowner John King told a fantastic story. The Kings lived at Thissellwold, the estate that is now Winthrop Hall. Accompanied by her cousin and a maid, the young girl ventured to nearby Witches' Woods for a picnic. Although they'd visited the spot many times, they got lost coming home.

According to the young girl's account: *"They suddenly came upon a ridge and looked down to behold an old Colonial farmhouse which they approached to get directions home. However, whenever they neared the house, it would disappear. They finally returned home, confused and frightened."* (1962 archives, Endicott College).

As the Kings were respected members of the community, the story was widely reported.

The pink lady, I soon learned, was far from elusive. People advised me to get in touch with Sally King, a Beverly resident and former Endicott Dean of Students from 1971 to '80. Upon hearing about my mission, King was not only willing to talk about the ghost, she was eager. Ironically, she had encountered the ghost at a Halloween party hosted by a group of Winthrop Hall students.

It was late afternoon when King, accompanied by College Registrar Barbara Decker, arrived at Winthrop Hall. The pair were directed downstairs to the recreation room. While they were enjoying the refreshments and Halloween decorations, their attention was diverted. King remembers the incident distinctly: "I swear to God, it was a ghost, an apparition, coming down the stairs. All of a sudden there it was, close by and wearing a pink dress."

Both women witnessed the vision. "It wasn't tangible, it was as if it was made of smoke, although every detail was perfectly clear." King shakes her head in wonder. "It was the most fascinating thing I've ever seen."

Although I've never been known for my fearlessness (I was too chicken to see "The Exorcist" when it first came out), I made an exception for the Winthrop Hall ghost. After all, the consensus among those who'd "met" her was that she was a friendly ghost.

Thus It was a dark and cloudy December afternoon when I visited Winthrop Hall. The students were away on winter break, leaving me free to roam the building. Before dropping me off with a key, the security guard reminded me that I'd be alone in the house.

"That's what I want," I said, with a jaunty wave. I stood outside for a long moment looking up at the mansion's vast stucco exterior. Finally, it was time to explore.

Humming to myself, I unlocked the heavy wooden door. In the foyer, I spotted the notorious painting of the tree and pond. There was nothing sinister about it. In fact, it looked like something you'd find at a local yard sale.

I decided to start at the top and work my way down. Thus I slowly climbed the stairs to the third floor. Hugging myself against the late afternoon chill, I headed down the long corridor, passing doors hung with holiday decorations. In the fading light, they did not cheer me.

A tall window at the end of the corridor cast a thin winter's glow. I stood before it, gazing down at the long verandah where Eleanor Tupper's daughter reportedly spotted the ghost. Ahead stretched a wide gray sea interrupted by jagged rocks, the same that, according to legend, had wrecked the sailor's ship.

I imagined the early occupants of the house observing the same view, unchanged all these decades. As I stood lost in thought, I became aware of a distant sound, a tinkling of chimes or bells. The sprawling house suddenly felt smaller. I had the feeling I was not alone.

I glanced behind me. Why hadn't I brought someone with me–my 100 pound black Lab, for instance? I scanned the wall for a light switch. It was at the other end of the corridor, which suddenly seemed very long indeed. I headed toward it, walking faster with each step. Soon I was scurrying so fast I feared losing my shoes. Each door I passed was a blur until I finally reached the stairs, taking them two at a time.

I didn't pause in the foyer. Instead I marched to the door and yanked it open. Before slamming it behind me, I got a glimpse of the painting: It was hanging upside down . . .

Outside, an early twilight had descended. I was halfway up the driveway when I dared turn for a final look. A curtain in an upper window moved. Was it a draft or my imagination? I decided to leave it a mystery . . .

The End

www.ingramcontent.com/pod-product-compliance
Lightning Source LLC
Chambersburg PA
CBHW030615130626
46552CB00002B/570